A ROOM WHERE

THE STAR-SPANGLED BANNER

CANNOT BE HEARD

A NOVEL IN THREE PARTS

A ROOM WHERE
THE STAR-SPANGLED BANNER
CANNOT BE HEARD

LEVY HIDEO

TRANSLATED BY CHRISTOPHER D. SCOTT

COLUMBIA UNIVERSITY PRESS

NEW YORK

COLUMBIA UNIVERSITY PRESS

PUBLISHERS SINCE 1893

NEW YORK   CHICHESTER, WEST SUSSEX

Original title: Seijōki no kikoenai heya
Copyright © Hideo Levy 1992
Originally published in Japan in 1992 by Kodansha, Tokyo.
English translation © Christopher D. Scott 2011

This book has been selected by the Japanese Literature Publishing Project (JLPP),
an initiative of the Agency for Cultural Affairs of Japan.

Library of Congress Cataloging-in-Publication Data
Levy, Ian Hideo, 1950–
[Seijōki no kikoenai heya. English]
A room where the Star-Spangled Banner cannot be heard : a novel in three parts / by Levy
Hideo; translated by Christopher D. Scott.
p. cm.
ISBN 978-0-231-15744-5 (cloth : acid-free paper) — ISBN 978-0-231-52797-2 (electronic)
1. Americans—Japan—Fiction. 2. Nineteen sixties—Fiction. 3. Self-realization—
Fiction. 4. Yokohama-shi (Japan)—Fiction. 5. Tokyo (Japan)—Fiction. I. Scott,
Christopher D., 1971– II. Title.
PS3562.E927177S4513   2011
895.6'35—dc22
2010044577

♾

Columbia University Press books are printed on permanent and durable acid-free paper.
This book was printed on paper with recycled content.
Printed in the United States of America

c 10 9 8 7 6 5 4 3 2 1

References to Internet Web sites (URLs) were accurate at the time of writing.
Neither the author nor Columbia University Press is responsible for URLs that may have expired
or changed since the manuscript was prepared.

CONTENTS

v

TRANSLATOR'S INTRODUCTION

Levy Hideo, the Japanese pen name of Ian Hideo Levy, is the first white American novelist to write in Japanese. By writing in a language not his own, or at least not the one he was born into, Levy follows in the footsteps of many other authors who have written in a language that is not their mother tongue. In English, Joseph Conrad and Vladimir Nabokov are perhaps the most famous examples, but there are many others, especially postcolonial or diasporic writers such as Chinua Achebe and Eva Hoffman. Even in Japan, there is a long history of ethnically non-Japanese writers writing in Japanese, mostly Korean residents of Japan (so-called *zainichi* Koreans) and other colonial subjects and their descendants. This large and diverse body of writing has been called "Japanese-language literature" (*Nihongo bungaku*), as opposed to "Japanese literature" (*Nihon bungaku*), which assumes a natural or seamless correlation among Japanese nationality, Japanese ethnicity, Japanese language, and Japanese culture. Levy's work shatters this equation, showing that the Japanese language and Japanese literature do not belong solely to the Japanese nation or the Japanese people. To this extent, his work should be understood as a form of "Japanese-language literature," which was originally a product of Japanese imperialism and colonialism. Though not a colonial or postcolonial writer in the traditional sense of the term, Levy is part of what might be called a spectrum of "*zainichi*" writers, or writers who reside in Japan and write in Japanese but who do not necessarily identify as Japanese or possess Japanese nationality. Thus, it is only fitting that his debut novel, *A Room Where the Star-Spangled Banner Cannot Be Heard* (Seijōki no kikoenai heya, 1992), should appear in English from Columbia University Press, which has published translations of other important works of "Japanese-language literature" in recent years, such as Wu Zhouliu's *Orphan of Asia* (Ajia no koji, 1945) and Kim Sŏk-pŏm's *The Curious Tale of Mandogi's Ghost* (Mandogi yūrei kitan, 1970).[1] Levy's novel represents a new kind of "Japanese-language literature" and a new direction for Japanese literature in general.

But there is a critical distinction between these earlier examples of "Japanese-language literature" and Levy's work. Unlike Taiwanese colonial subjects like Wu Zhouliu and *zainichi* Koreans like Kim Sŏkpŏm, who had no choice but to learn and write in Japanese as a result of Japanese colonial rule, Levy did have a choice. He could either write in English, his native language, or write in Japanese, his adopted mother tongue. In this regard at least, Levy occupies a position of privilege compared to earlier "Japanese-language literature" writers, who were forced to become Japanese and use Japanese. Still, why would a white American writer like Levy choose to write in a foreign language like Japanese? This question assumes that only Japanese people can or should write in Japanese. Obviously, Levy's work challenges this assumption. His work also raises the more interesting question: what if Japanese chose him, not the other way around? That is to say, what if Levy's particular set of personal and historical circumstances made it unavoidable—perhaps even necessary—for him to live in Japan and write in Japanese? If so, then what does his work say about the relationship among language, identity, and experience? Finally, what does it mean to translate his work (back) into English, the language that Levy and his protagonist Ben Isaac have tried so hard to escape—or to forget, as one scene in the novel describes it—in the search for a room of their own, as it were, in Japan and the Japanese language? What does it mean to read *A Room Where the Star-Spangled Banner Cannot Be Heard* in English, or in the United States in particular? These are some of the questions I will address in this brief introduction. Levy's work, I believe, has wide-ranging implications, not only for redefining what we think of as "Japan" or "Japanese literature" but also for broadening the definition of "America" and "American literature."

Like the protagonist of this novel, Levy has spent most of his life outside of America. Born in 1950 to a Jewish father and a Polish mother in Berkeley, California, Levy grew up in many places: the United States, Taiwan, Hong Kong, and eventually Japan, where he went to live with his father in the American consulate in Yokohama at the age of seventeen. His middle name, Hideo, came from his father's Japanese American friend who was sent to an internment camp during World War II. The pen name Levy Hideo, a hybrid of English and Japanese, thus reflects his transnational and multilingual upbringing; it bears the traces of multiple languages and multiple diasporas. While living in Yokohama, Levy began learning Japanese and reading Japanese literature in English translation, much like Ben does in this novel. Levy continued his studies at Princeton University, eventually earning a doctorate there and joining the faculty as an assistant professor of Japanese literature in 1978. In 1981, he published a translation of the first five volumes of Japan's earliest imperial poetry anthology, *The Ten Thousand Leaves* (Man'yōshū, ca. 759), which won a National Book Award for Translation the following year. During the 1980s and early 1990s, while teaching at Princeton and Stanford universities, Levy split his time between Japan and the United States and began writing in Japanese more and more. The result was this novel, which was published in three parts in the leading Japanese literary journal *Gunzō* between 1987 and 1991. In 1991, he quit his tenured position at Stanford and moved to Japan permanently to pursue a writing career. The following year, *A*

Room Where the Star-Spangled Banner Cannot Be Heard won the Noma Literary Award for New Writers, thus establishing him as an up-and-coming writer in Japan. Japanese writers and critics widely praised the novel, with the soon-to-be Nobel Prize winner Ōe Kenzaburō calling it "a superior symbol of mutual understanding between two languages and two nations [kokumin]."[2] Since then, Levy has written many more works of fiction and nonfiction that have come to symbolize a new style of writing—so-called "border-crossing literature" (ekkyō bungaku)—that spans different languages and nations. His major works include the novellas Tiananmen (Ten'anmon, 1996), which was nominated for the prestigious Akutagawa Prize, and Ode to the Nation (Kokumin no uta, 1997), as well as various essay collections and interviews. He also has won a number of important Japanese literary awards, including the Ōsaragi Jirō Prize for Thousands and Thousands of Pieces (Chiji ni kudakete, 2004), the first novel in Japanese to deal with the events of 9/11, and the Itō Sei Prize for Fake Water (Kari no mizu, 2008), which is set in contemporary China. Since Tiananmen, much of Levy's work has been about the reality (and surreality) of life in mainland China, where he has traveled extensively, mapping out new frontiers for the Japanese language and Japanese literature.

As this brief biography suggests, Levy writes in Japanese to explore and articulate his own identity, which has been deeply intertwined with Japan and the Japanese language. As he notes in the afterword to the paperback edition of A Room Where the Star-Spangled Banner Cannot Be Heard, had he written this novel in English, it would have been just an English translation of a Japanese novel. He felt he had no choice but to write it in Japanese because so much of his life was experienced in Japan and in Japanese.[3] This does not mean, however, that Levy's work is simply about "becoming Japanese" or "going native." Writing in Japanese and being (or becoming) Japanese are two very different things, as the history of "Japanese-language literature" so vividly illustrates. It would be more accurate to say that Levy's work is about the struggle or productive tension between writing in Japanese and not being Japanese, or the dilemma of being a writer of Japanese but not a Japanese writer. Here lies the real power and significance of his literary project: it demonstrates that one does not have to be Japanese in order to write or have a voice in Japanese. Of course, many earlier works of "Japanese-language literature" made a similar point, but they were products of Japanese colonialism, which used the exact same logic to assimilate and oppress colonial subjects. As the first non-Japanese and non-Asian to write literature in Japanese, Levy has paved the way for many other writers—Japanese and non-Japanese alike—to express themselves in Japanese. Indeed, he was the first of a new generation of transcultural and multilingual writers who are literally changing the face of Japanese literature. They include Tawada Yōko, Mizumura Minae, Yang Yi, Shirin Nezammafi, and Wen Youren, who are producing works in Japanese and other languages (like German, English, and Chinese) that radically question the connections (or disconnections) among race, ethnicity, nationality, and language. In retrospect, then, *A Room Where the Star-Spangled Banner Cannot Be Heard* was a landmark text. To many readers of Japanese, including this translator, it opened up new horizons of possibility for the Japanese language and Japanese literature. At the same time, it signaled the end of an era in Japan, exemplified by the death of the Shōwa emperor (Hirohito) in 1989 and the bursting of the so-called "bubble economy" in the early 1990s, two monumental events that underwrite this work in many ways.

While *A Room Where the Star-Spangled Banner Cannot Be Heard* is clearly informed by postwar Japanese history and postwar Japanese literature through its explicit references to the student protests against the U.S.–Japan Security Treaty (ANPO) during the 1960s and its knowing nods to postwar writers like Mishima Yukio, Ōe Kenzaburō, and Nakagami Kenji, it also looks back at postwar America and the sense of loss and disillusionment that the 1960s brought about. It is an elegy to a lost home, a requiem for a missing mother tongue. From the death of John F. Kennedy to the ravages of the Vietnam War, or from the shouts of "Yankee, go home!" outside the American consulate in Yokohama to the public and private tears of two women in Arlington, Virginia, this story traces the crisis or breakdown of American national, social, and cultural identity during the 1960s. In other words, it is as much about postwar America as it is about postwar Japan. This is why it is so important to translate this novel (back) into English, Levy's native language, and to read it in the United States, where Levy was born. Through the mirror of translation, it allows us to see the English language and the United States from a more non-native or denationalized perspective. It makes us all foreigners for a while, reminding us of the otherness of English, not to mention Japanese, and the unfamiliarity of the places and identities we call home. Indeed, it makes us all *gaijin* (outsiders), a term that encompasses immigrants, aliens, strangers, refugees, fugitives, freaks, and anyone else who does not belong or fit in. At the same time, the novel also asks us to reconsider the relationship between "Japanese literature" and "American literature," and to see how Levy's work both bridges and transcends these categories. Just as the voices of Mishima, Ōe, and Nakagami whisper through these pages, there are echoes of American writers here as well: Walt Whitman, James Baldwin, Philip Roth, and many others. In this way, the novel lies somewhere between Japanese literature and American literature, somewhere between Japan and the United States. Therefore, *A Room Where the Star-Spangled Banner Cannot Be Heard* will always be lost in translation, as the cliché goes, never fully at home or completely comfortable (i.e., "native") in Japanese or in English. The title, which is long and somewhat awkward or foreign-sounding in either language, is a perfect example of this. In my translation, I have tried to convey a sense of the "foreignness" or untranslatability of Levy's prose, which has a beauty and a rhythm all its own.

A ROOM WHERE

THE STAR-SPANGLED BANNER

CANNOT BE HEARD

A ROOM WHERE

THE STAR SPANGLED BANNER

CANNOT BE HEARD

I

BEYOND THE PARK, THE PIER FELL SILENT AS ONE BY ONE, the warehouse lights above the choppy water went out. The Stars and Stripes, illuminated by four floodlights, waved in the night wind off the harbor. Slowly, the flag was lowered by two U.S. Marines, with their impeccable white gloves, who folded it neatly. When the floodlights were turned off, the windows in the residence on the second floor of the consulate went dark as well.

Ben Isaac had been watching the scene unfold from the middle window, framed by two columns supporting the portico. Now in the darkness he slipped on a blue jacket and stepped onto the dimly lit stairwell landing. He crept down the cold marble staircase to the first-floor hallway. At the far end was the front door, all mahogany and copper. With both hands, he yanked the door open.

In the front yard, he was in plain sight of the Japanese guardsmen at the sentry box, but the guards turned a blind eye to him, probably because they were afraid of saying anything to the consul's son. But as he left the grounds and headed for the streets of Yokohama, he could feel their silent gaze on his back.

He checked to be sure he had the three thousand yen and his ID with an eagle stamped above his face, then crossed Yamashita Park Avenue and followed the sidewalk along the park's iron fence. Inside the park, shadowy figures roamed over the patchy grass—vagrants, probably, looking for a place to sleep. Every so often, a tentative voice called out to him from the darkness. *Harro*. Ben Isaac didn't know how to respond.

Across the street, a dozen taxis were lined up, waiting for customers. Sailors, their white uniforms soiled, had gathered outside the U.S. Navy Club. The light from the street lamps made their crew-cut heads look yellow and revealed a bottle of bourbon being passed from white hand to black hand. They scowled at the few passing cars, looking like they wanted to curse at them, if only they knew how to in Japanese. . . . It was another night in Yokohama, late autumn 1967.

At seventeen, Ben was only two or three years younger than these sailors. Unlike them, though, Ben wore his wispy blond hair down to his bony shoulders. He stuck to the park side of the street, hoping to avoid the sailors' eyes and trying not to listen to the soulful voice of James Brown oozing out the open door of the club.

By the time he got to the Hongkong and Shanghai Bank, the song in his mother tongue had faded away. So had the shadows inside the iron fence. Ben slowed down. From his jacket pocket, he took out a crumpled Wakaba cigarette and lit up. He stepped into the plaza in front of the Silk Hotel, weaving through the cold, intersecting beams of car headlights.

At the next corner, he turned onto a wide, tree-lined street called Japan Grand Avenue. It was more than twice as wide as the one he had just walked down. Ben remembered his father saying that during the Meiji era this used to be the boundary between the foreign settlement and the Japanese district. At the moment, there was no one crossing the street. The lights were off in the prefectural office building, which loomed on the other side. With no cars in sight, Japan Grand Avenue was deathly quiet. Overhead stretched a jet-black sky, ready to swallow the young white boy beneath it.

Ben crossed to the other side and slipped in between the two rows of gingko trees that bordered the prefectural office. Moving farther away from the streetlights, he disappeared into a tangle of shadows beneath the barren limbs.

By the time he arrived at Sakuragichō Station, the milk bar and the shoeshine stand were closed, and only one window at the ticket counter was open. He passed through the rundown terminal and boarded a Tōyoko Line express train for Tokyo. The second he stepped on the train, he breathed a sigh of relief. There were no passengers in the car.

From the loudspeaker came a crackling voice: *Ma mo naku* . . . "In a few moments . . ." Ben couldn't catch the rest of it.

Soon after the train pulled out of the station, it began a gentle uphill climb, sending vibrations through Ben's scrawny legs as he sat in a corner of the car. As it picked up speed along the elevated track, he looked backward and gazed at the city lights spreading out like a galaxy. He felt a little dizzy.

Ben's eyes drank in their first full view of a Japanese city at night. Unlike during the day, the outlines of the buildings blurred, and everywhere he looked neon signs squirmed quietly in *kana* and *kanji*. They reflected the dreams and ailments of the city in colors to match: WHISKY, PHARMACEUTICALS, TURKISH BATH, and CLINIC. From station to station, they transmitted the city's secrets, which were not meant for the eyes of a young boy from *somewhere else*.

Indeed, Ben couldn't read most of the characters. And even if he could, he could not fully understand what they meant. For Ben was still a traveler who could barely read road signs. In Yokohama the train started gradually to fill with passengers. Some looked on him with pity, others with ridicule, others with shock, discovering in Ben's intense blue-gray eyes a burning desire to know the world around him.

Ben was accustomed to such stares. The son of an American diplomat, he had grown up as a white child in Asia during the 1950s, changing homes and countries every few years since infancy: Hong Kong, Phnom Penh, Taipei. . . .

Blond kids in Asia grow up under the gaze of many people. Walking through the narrow alleyways of the market, Ben attracted a following of barefooted boys his age who would shout out, in Chinese, words like "America" (well-meant) or "white devil" (less so). When he returned to his house, which was surrounded by a thick wall topped with shards of colored glass to discourage burglars, the two tall security guards and the three servant *yongren* took turns giving him piggyback rides. In the mornings, he went to school on a rickshaw with its shades pulled up and the adults by the roadside staring at him.

In Taiwan, he attended a red brick missionary school that rose like a floating fortress from the rice paddies shimmering in the tropical sun. There he learned English; American history; the language spoken by the farmers, who glared at the school while they worked; and stories from the illustrated Bible. His teacher was a white-haired minister who had been born near the end of the Qing dynasty and lived his entire life in Asia. After prayer in the afternoons, the minister would point to the horizon, where farmers plowed the paddies with water buffaloes and clouds were stacked like a majestic staircase leading up to an ancient city of gold. There, the minister said, lay the real "promised land of Jerusalem, the Shining City on a Hill," just like in the pictures from the Book of Revelation.

By the time he was ten years old, Ben knew that wherever he lived, outside the walls of his home would always be markets filled with young boys in ragtag clothing and roadsides thronged with brown-skinned adults—just as there would always be tall security guards at his house, farmers plowing rice paddies, and simplistic religious beliefs taught at the missionary school.

Six months before he was to graduate from elementary school, his mother suddenly took him away to live in a house where there were no security guards and no *yongren*—and no father. His mother's house was located across the river from Washington, D.C., near the national cemetery, on a street in a poor white neighborhood of working-class families who had drifted there from the Southern United States. The whitewashed porch opened onto a small parlor, which was dominated by a huge black-and-white Westinghouse television set. The room was decorated with Oriental antiques, which his mother had brought back from his father's collection. Surrounded by porcelain bowls and teak Buddhas, Ben and his mother would watch *The Lucy Show* and the *CBS Evening News*.

Around the time they got word his father had been appointed consul in Yokohama, Ben's mother found a job in Washington and Ben entered high school in Virginia. As he sat on the top step of the porch, waiting for his mother to come home from work, Ben sometimes recalled the tropical afternoon clouds he would stare at from the red brick missionary school. Before he knew it, that Shining City on a Hill vanished, and by the time he graduated from high school, the Asia of his childhood was nothing more than bits and pieces of a vivid memory from long ago.

After the second station past Yokohama, the passengers seemed to stop looking at Ben, perhaps because their curiosity had worn out. He couldn't read anything from their faces except fatigue from a long day's work. Ben shifted his gaze back to the window and the night scene pressing against it. For Ben, who had just finished high school in America, *this* was the real New World: a Japanese city inlaid with pearly lights stretching from the foot of the mountains to the shores of the bay. As he looked down at the lanes, the alleys, and the back streets passing before him, he imagined throwing himself into that glittering maze and escaping his father's wrath. Speeding over the sea of lights, the train transported Ben farther and farther away from the port of Yokohama and the mansion where his father lived.

With a roar, the train barreled across a bridge and into Tokyo.

IT WAS SUMMER. A PSYCHEDELIC SONG THAT WAS ALL THE rage that summer, when he left America, ran through his head:

Cocaine—
Cocaine

Ben was aboard a large passenger ship. It was dusk. The ship had set sail for Yokohama that day.

running 'round my heart,
running 'round my brain

The previous night, he had stood on the wharf in Honolulu. Behind a truck that blocked the light from the loading dock, Ben had tried drugs for the first time in his life. The guy said it was hashish mixed with mescaline. When Ben woke up the next morning, the song was still ringing in his ears. In fact, it was "running 'round" his brain all day long. Even at the end of the day, he couldn't get it out of his head.

It was the summer of 1967. The sound of the waves slapping against the ship's hull added a weird rhythm to the song.

Crouching beneath one of the big bald eagles emblazoned on the funnels of the SS *President Roosevelt*, Ben gazed alone at the evening sun quietly sinking into the vast ocean.

Cocaine—
Ah, bittersweet!

Ben recalled a similar scene from his childhood. It was an image of the evening sun over the midsummer strait.

A fleet of patrol boats was anchored on the horizon. They were bobbing up and down like the tiny heads of swimmers treading water, unable to make it back to shore.

He was in the back seat of a jeep, listening to the lapping of the waves on the shore and the howling of the wind through the brambles of barbed wire stretching in either direction.

Beneath these sounds, he could make out the fluttering of a Republic of China Naval Jack hoisted above the barbed wire and the grunting of pigs from a nearby village.

Everyone was speechless before the brilliant orange sunset over the Taiwan Strait.

The sunlight streaming through the windshield was blinding. From the back seat, Ben observed the sweat matting his father's hair, making it look thinner than it already was.

His father began whispering in a language Ben didn't understand. He guessed it was a dialect of Chinese, filled as it was with strange syllables and intonations. And then his father wrapped his arm slowly but surely, like the ponderous leaves of a tropical plant, around the shoulders of the woman in the passenger seat.

Ben knew the woman well. His father had told him to call her *jiejie*, the word for "big sis" in the Beijing dialect. Jiejie glanced back at Ben nervously several times, then stopped, perhaps reassured by whatever it was his father had said.

Ben gazed out from the jeep desperately. His eyes moved from the barbed wire down to the beach and across the ripples of the ebbing tide. Finally, he fixed his gaze upon the orange horizon and held it there indefinitely.

Come here, Mama, come on quick—
Cocaine's making your poor boy sick

A single reconnaissance plane flew across the setting sun. It was headed to China. The roar of the plane faded, leaving behind an all-encompassing silence.

Ben wanted to scream, but he was overwhelmed by the silence, which was greater than any yell a young boy could muster. He shut his eyes.

It was later that same year, one week after John F. Kennedy won the U.S. presidential election, that Ben and his mother boarded the SS *President Wilson* at Keelung and returned "home" to an America that felt like a foreign country.

THE EARLY MORNING SKY WOKE BEN UP. HE WAS IN A four-and-a-half–mat tatami room, surrounded by gray walls and a yellowed shoji screen faintly visible in the pale light. How long had he been asleep? The window had no curtains, and he could see the vague outline of the persimmon tree, whose upper branches seemed to have crept up the earthen wall to the second floor. Persimmons dangled in midair, waxy in the dim light.

The sky began to turn a deep blue. From somewhere in the distance, toward the city's invisible horizon, came the sound of the first train, cutting through the chill of dawn. Ben shuddered for a moment under his flimsy quilt.

"Andō . . ."

Ben's friend was sleeping beside him, his legs thrust under a small desk, completely oblivious to the back-and-forth between dream and reality in Ben's mind. His friend's face was round and naïve-looking, like that of a young farmer, but it had the sort of sallow complexion of a city dweller. His expression gave no indication that he had heard Ben call his name.

Ben sat up in the semidarkness and looked around. Something shimmered on the desk. Andō's flute. He had neglected to put it back in the case. A black school uniform hung on a plastic hanger. Above, a maroon university pennant and a photograph were tacked to the wall. The photograph, which seemed to have been torn from a magazine, was of a short, muscular man in a military uniform. Andō had said it was a famous author.

Next to the flute sat a square bottle, dimly reflecting the early morning light. On the label he could make out the letters NIKKA and the face of a white man with a red beard. Another white man hiding out in a place like this! Ben examined the label more closely: the tipsy white man was holding a glass of whisky and was wearing one of those puffy stand-up collars from the seventeenth century. The man reminded Ben of those Dutchmen who had come to Japan during the Edo era, venturing from trading posts on Dejima into Nagasaki, where the kids called them names like "ogre" and "long-nosed goblin." Those *kapitein* couldn't understand a thing and just stood there wide-eyed and dumb-faced. We're here, we're really *here*, they marveled, as though drunk. . . . Ben rubbed his eyes and realized that the crumpled blue mass beside the whisky bottle was his jacket.

Last night, the silver express train had slipped into a station under a sign that read SHIBUYA in *hiragana*. Ben got off the train and took a series of stairs and passageways through the station before changing to a long green train. Two stations later, a drunk, about the same age as Ben's father, got on. "Hey, *ketō*," the man shouted, using a derogatory term for Westerners. Ben moved to the next car. At the fifth stop, he leaped off the train like a white house mouse coughed up from the belly of a snake. As he stood alone in the crowd on the platform, he was met with a cold wind and a crush of eyes: the people jumping on and off the trains would stare at him for a moment before always looking away. Feeling overwhelmed, he pointed his feet in the direction of the stairs marked EXIT in English and in *kanji*.

On the main drag, he headed straight for the narrow slopes and alleys crowded with student boardinghouses and wooden apartment buildings. He was surprised by how well he knew the way. Each time he crossed an intersection, he avoided the side of the street with a police box. After two shrines and three public baths, the avenue headed downhill. At the bottom, he turned into an alley, which led to an even narrower alley. Finally he reached the last alley, where he slipped behind a house and ducked into a wooden apartment building. On the second floor, he knocked gently on the door at the end of the hallway.

In broken but insistent Japanese, he tried to tell his only friend in Tokyo about the situation at home—which he couldn't really explain in English, either—by piecing together fragments of words he had picked up from him. In the end, though, he simply mumbled, "I, uh, ran away from home."

Andō Yoshiharu listened without saying a word.

Ben stared at Andō's round face and unfashionably square haircut and imagined he could see the meaning of his own words slowly taking shape inside Andō's head.

A full three seconds passed before Andō suddenly burst out laughing. "Dude, you fought with your old man again?"

Perplexed that Andō's response should be laughter, Ben could only reply, "Yes, that's right."

"But how'd you get here by yourself . . . ? Well, never mind, you can crash here."

"Really?"

"Yeah, don't worry about it."

Andō reached up to the wooden shelf above his desk and brought down two glasses from behind a jumble of packs of Wakaba cigarettes he'd won at *pachinko* and a kettle and teacups—things he'd brought with him from the Aichi countryside when he moved to Tokyo for college last spring. After they knocked back a few whiskies together, Andō spread out his futon for Ben. For his own bed, Andō stuck his long legs under the desk and stretched out right on top of the adjacent tatami mat. He was asleep in no time.

After Andō had fallen asleep, Ben listened to the sound of the wind rustling through the upper branches of the persimmon tree. He rolled over and faced the gray wall, turning away from Andō's serene face, which he'd heard a female foreign student once describe as "like the Amida Buddha incarnate." In the dead silence of the four-and-a-half–mat room, he tossed and turned until dawn, chased by vivid dreams in three different languages.

Ben got up from the floor and grabbed his jacket from the desk. Then he stepped out into the hallway, carefully closing the door behind him, and tiptoed down the long, dark corridor. Passing a number of other doors, he came to a small kitchen at the top of the stairs. He took the stairs one at a time, feeling his way along the wall covered with old newspapers.

The first floor was completely quiet as well. As Ben headed for the front door, he passed a cracked mirror hanging above an old washbasin. In the metal frame, jagged pieces of glass were held together, just barely, by yellow tape the color of soiled bandages. In the mirror, Ben's reflection was a bizarre jigsaw puzzle left unfinished, the bits and pieces of pale flesh not quite matching.

Ben called to mind the different words he used for himself: the "I" and "me" he had been using since childhood, the *watakushi* and *boku* he learned when he started studying Japanese at age seventeen, and the *ore* he started using after he met Andō. None of them seemed to fit the fractured face he saw in the mirror. He moved slightly, and a thin ray of light shot through the dust-filled air and glimmered across the broken glass.

Where, Father, where?

He felt himself being drawn to a place somewhere beyond the distorted light. However, the more he peered at his reflection in the glass, the more he realized that behind every name he used for himself was nothing but emptiness. He became frightened. He looked away and hurried toward the front door.

In the predawn darkness of the alley, he braced himself against the cold.

2

The American consulate in Yokohama was destroyed in the Great Kantō Earthquake of 1923. When it was rebuilt, it was designed to be a smaller version of the White House. Behind the massive mahogany-and-copper front door, the first floor consisted of offices while the second floor, with its high ceilings and big picture windows, served as the consular residence. It was late in the year after John F. Kennedy's presidential election that Consul Jacob Isaac moved in with his young Chinese wife, Gui-lan, and their new baby boy. The parlor and dining room, which faced Yamashita Park Avenue, had the kind of plush indigo carpet popular among the American upper classes before the Second World War. The upholstery on the sofas and armchairs was in a gaudy pattern of flowers and birds.

The consular residence was three or four times bigger than Ben's mother's house in Virginia. According to the visitation rights agreed upon in family court, Ben was to live with his father after graduating from high school. Ben hadn't seen his father in seven years. Their reunion came with one condition: Ben was to return to America after one year and enter college. The government paid for his travel expenses as a "dependent visitor," a status it had set up to deal with such cases, which were especially common in the Far East. The summer of his seventeenth year, Ben came to Yokohama on the SS *President Roosevelt* from San Francisco via Honolulu.

When he arrived at his father's residence, Ben was given the bedroom between the parlor and his father's study. The room was directly above the front entrance. If this were the real White House, Gui-lan explained to him on his first day there, his room would be diagonally across from the Lincoln Bedroom. Her English had improved a great deal since the time he used to call her Jiejie. Gui-lan had never seen the real White House, but now that she was ensconced as the lady of the house, she knew the consulate inside and out.

Ben's room had a window with Venetian blinds. When he pulled the blinds, he could see the American flag flying right outside his window—from the minute the consulate opened in the morning to the moment the lights went out at night. Like a dazzling screen, the Stars and Stripes blocked out all other scenery. Every so often, depending on the wind, it would offer a fleeting glimpse of the dense treetops in Yamashita Park or the funnels of the passenger ships docked at the pier.

To take in the scenery fully, Ben had first to pass through his father's study in the adjoining room, which was lined with musty tomes like a Meiji-era English translation of Confucius' *Analects*, *The Writings of Lafcadio Hearn*, and James Murdoch's *A History of Japan*. Arranged among the books were Oriental antiques: a yellowed *netsuke*, a Bizen-ware teacup, a white porcelain Goddess of Mercy, a potbellied Buddha from Taiwan. Where the bookshelves ended, a door led to the main staircase. Late at night, after his father and Gui-lan put his black-haired little brother to bed and retired to their bedroom at the back of the residence, Ben would sneak across his father's study, climb the marble staircase past the portraits of Townsend Harris and the successive American consuls to Japan that adorned the walls of the landing, and go out onto the roof.

From there, he could see all of Yamashita Park Avenue. The avenue, which ran straight in either direction, was a curious one. Seemingly suspended between the nineteenth and twentieth centuries, it did not belong to any country. The buildings on the consulate side of the street included the Silk Hotel, the Hongkong and Shanghai Bank, the U.S. Navy Club, a British trading firm sequestered behind a red brick wall, and the Hotel New Grand, which General MacArthur had allegedly used as a headquarters when he first came to Japan during the Occupation.

On the opposite side of the street, crowds of Japanese strolled through the park by day. On summer nights, men in short-sleeved dress shirts and women in white dresses could be seen under the pale light of paper lanterns hanging from the trees. Some nights, the faint sounds of people laughing in Japanese would cross the avenue. Like the briny smell of the sea, wisps of words Ben couldn't comprehend would be carried in on the night wind off the harbor. At such moments, as he gazed down at the figures of Japanese briefly appearing under the white light of the lanterns before disappearing beneath the dark canopy of trees, he would be filled with an emotion somewhere between longing and loneliness, as though he were seeing a *tableau vivant* in someone else's dream.

SUNDAYS BROUGHT THE GREATEST NUMBER OF JAPANESE to the park.

Surrounded by a tall iron fence, the consulate reeked of extraterritoriality, but the scene on the sidewalk was a reminder to all inside, if they'd forgotten, that this was Japan after all. From morning to night there were outdoor stalls offering lemon-lime soda called *ramune*, goldfish-scooping games called *kingyo-sukui*, and grilled corn on the cob called *tōmorokoshi*. Japanese families poured out from the park onto both sides of the avenue. Apparently, the consulate, being a miniature White House, was one of Yokohama's famous sites imbued with "an air of exoticism," so the couples and groups of female students who were milling about would stop in front of the iron fence to peek in or take a snapshot.

Ben greeted each Sunday with mixed emotions. The day was, as it was for the Japanese, a time for family outings. Following behind his father and Gui-lan, Ben—with four-year-old Jeffrey in tow—would march through the outer gate of the consulate and walk down the crowded sidewalk along Yamashita Park Avenue to a hotel, where they would have Sunday brunch. The restaurant was on the hotel's fifth floor, and it was always full of American families who'd just been to church. After being seen to their reserved table near the window, they placed their orders: omelets for his father and Gui-lan, pancakes for Ben and Jeffrey.

As his father and Gui-lan started to speak in her native Shanghainese, Ben checked out the other families seated at tables around them. All of them—the men in charcoal gray or brown suits and their wives in genteel dresses, some with red or yellow rose corsages—were white, and all spoke in English (many with a Midwestern accent or a Southern twang). Their young sons, in sky-blue blazers and stifling bow ties, and their young daughters, in garish Sunday dresses and with their long brown hair tied with rainbow-colored ribbons, were like clones of their parents. Ben remembered that when he was Jeffrey's age, he also used to dine with his father and mother at hotel restaurants, in Jakarta and Phnom Penh, where the only other customers were Americans and Europeans. Now his family was so utterly different from the ones around him.

"*Omelette du jour,*" the Japanese waitress pronounced flawlessly, placing two pillowy omelets on white Noritake china in front of his father and Gui-lan. It was then that Ben noticed a middle-aged couple at the next table staring at them. The woman, like someone who had smelled a fart during High Mass, was showing her distinct displeasure at seeing Ben's father, who was nearly bald and without a coat and tie, and Gui-lan, who, at about thirty years old, was much younger and spoke in tones that didn't even sound like Japanese. Gui-lan, who had an oval face like the court singers in the illustrated woodblock-print novels from the Qing dynasty in Ben's father's study, was the only Oriental woman seated in the dining room. To make matters worse, she was dressed more formally than his father. The root of anxiety for this white woman living in Asia was sitting right in front of her eyes—

and eating an omelet, no less. When his father realized they were being stared at, he muttered with unmistakable disdain, "Damn Christians."

Jacob Isaac never wore a suit on Sunday. Nor had he once set foot inside a synagogue in the almost twenty years since his first diplomatic posting in Asia, which was in Shanghai on the eve of the Chinese Revolution, or so Ben's mother had said. When asked about his religion, Jacob would automatically reply, "We're Confucian." Ben's father had been born in Brooklyn, where he received an Orthodox Jewish education. His family reluctantly gave their consent when he married a Polish Catholic girl from West Virginia. When he divorced her ten years later, however, and married a Chinese woman nearly half his age, the Isaac clan saw this as an act of ethnic betrayal and cut ties with him completely. This too Ben learned from his mother. But he knew from personal experience that the sin of his father's transgression had been passed down to him. After his parents divorced, the letters from his paternal grandmother, his aunts and uncles, and his cousins suddenly stopped.

Ben, meanwhile, moved to Virginia with his mother. On the last day of a school trip to New York City during his freshman year in high school, when he was fourteen, Ben ducked into a subway phone booth and called his grandmother in Brooklyn. An old woman answered with a feeble hello. "It's Ben," he said. He heard nothing on the other end. To stop the flow of silence that began to fill the subterranean West Fourth Street phone booth like dirty rainwater, he added, "It's your grandson Ben, Jacob's son." A second later, his grandmother slammed the phone down.

At the entrance to the restaurant, American families mixed with naval officers in their dress whites as they waited for tables to open up. It was noon. Beneath the frosted glass of the picture window, which cut off the noise from the street and blocked out the strong August sunlight, crowds of Japanese people were streaming by.

The Isaac family got up to leave, exiting through the hotel's revolving door and turning right toward Marine Tower. They set off for Motomachi. The sun's rays were so intense that they decided to cross to the park side, where the outdoor stalls were, and walk under the shady canopy of trees. Suddenly they found themselves thrust into a mass of people surrounding the stalls. Ben was holding Jeffrey's hand. Each time they passed a stall, Jeffrey would yank Ben's hand and scream, "I want it!" "No!" Gui-lan would scream back, so loudly that people turned their heads. Even the crowds in Yokohama, so accustomed to seeing foreigners, stared at this family without compunction: at his father's bald head sticking up above the crowd, at Gui-lan walking close beside his father, at Ben with his long blond hair, and at Jeffrey tugging at Ben's hand.

They focused on Jeffrey first. His jet-black hair, like that of a Mongol, combined with his chiseled Hellenistic features brought squeals, from schoolgirls in particular, of *So cuuuute* and *Harro, harro.*

Then their attention—which had been fixed on the young boy of mixed blood—naturally shifted to Ben, who was holding the young boy's hand, then to Ben's father, and finally to Gui-lan, who was walking between Ben and his father but was closer in age to Ben. At this point, as though they had come to an illogical conclusion without realizing it, the squeals of delight abruptly stopped. A perplexed silence followed, punctuated by two or three giggles.

"Look!" his father exclaimed. "Those fools can't figure out who's who and how we're all related." He laughed loudly, more than he ever would have around white people. It was an unrestrained laugh that sounded like he had disgorged something vile from deep within his huge body.

Ben grasped the hand of the young boy who was Gui-lan's son and his own brother, feeling the sudden urge to kill his father. This thought crossed his mind like a cloud eclipsing the midday August sun. Then it was gone, replaced by a burning shame in his chest. Shame . . . suffocation from the schoolgirls' syrupy *harro*s from the next stall. . . . He wanted to tell it to someone, he wanted to scream it to someone.

But everyone around him was Japanese.

Over Sunday dinner toward the end of the month, Ben announced that he wanted to study Japanese at a university in Tokyo. Gui-lan expressed surprise, but reluctantly his father agreed after glancing at her at the other end of the table. "Well," he said, "it's not as beautiful as Chinese, but . . ."

Ben would take classes three times a week in a Japanese program at a private university in Tokyo that he had found himself. There was one condition, however: on the days Ben had class, he was to return to the consulate before dinnertime.

"No detours on your way home," his father warned. Then, winking at Gui-lan, he added, "Especially not to places like Shinjuku."

3

To reach the gates of manhood, according to a nineteenth-century poet Ben had read in high school, every young man must first pass through an endless maze of corridors. The corridors of Ben's youth were always filled with the echoes of adult footsteps, which cast long shadows on his memory.

There was the official government residence, where his father disappeared down a hallway with a briefcase of state documents handcuffed to his thick wrist, leaving Ben by the front door.

There was the dictator's palace in a tropical country, where Ben's parents paid their respects while Ben waited in a teak-floored hall, peering from behind a bluestone column at the peasants and the crippled tendering their supplications in silence, the smell of musk hanging in the air.

There was the U.S. Air Force base in another tropical country, where the daughters of peasants—who once stood in the shadows on the backstreets of the capital like "whores," as the rickshaw drivers would call them—now waited along the dark green walls for a flight to California, wearing curlers and cut-offs, with half-white or half-black babies in their arms.

There were the streets in Asia where Ben wandered alone, free from the grip of his parents. The narrow alley of a market he squeezed through as a hundred brown-skinned hands reached out to stroke his blond locks. The shopping arcade of the Imperial Hotel, with its glittering Buddhas and five-story pagodas in the souvenir shop.

There was the labyrinthine colonial estate in Taiwan that Japanese officials handed over to their American counterparts after the fall of the Greater Japanese Empire. The footsteps of *yongren* on the long veranda leading from his father's quarters to his mother's quarters. The *sumi-e* painting of a Japanese mountain temple complex shrouded in mist that the former owner—in a hurry to repatriate—had left behind in an alcove.

And, finally, there was the International Studies Center at W University, where Ben had been enrolled since mid-September. The yellow paint was peeling from the walls. Up the stairs and down the hall was the foreign students' lounge, where foreign students hung out on sofas and Japanese students stood, waiting for the chance to use their English. The foreign students mostly ignored them, but the Japanese students patiently stood their ground, like stony-faced imperial guards.

On a wall in the lounge, students had scrawled riotous things in English, like:

"GOD IS DEAD" —Nietzsche

And beneath that:

"NIETZSCHE IS DEAD" —God

It was something one might see under the arches of buildings or on bathroom walls at American universities.

One day, someone with a Kansas monotone announced, "God's not dead." It was a balding graduate student with a wiry goatee that looked like pubic hair. "He's just lost in Shinjuku Station."

That got a laugh from a couple of female students who were sitting on the sofa reading cartoons in *The New Yorker*. The Japanese students stood in silence, without a smile.

A girl who had been sitting in the corner—her platinum hair swept into a tight bun, her nose in a book—suddenly stood up, an annoyed look on her face, and strode over to the open window.

From somewhere on the vast university campus could be heard a growing roar. It sounded like hundreds of people chanting the slogans in unison, and as the crowd drew nearer, the chant became a battle cry: *Anpō funsai, Okinawa kaesē!* "Destroy ANPO,[1] return Okinawa!"

"Metaphysical jokes don't work in Japan—thank God," the girl mumbled out the window, as if the late afternoon shadows on the brick auditorium across the way were listening.

Ben had noticed her before. She always sat by herself, away from the other foreign students. He saw her reading Natsume Sōseki's *Kokoro* in Japanese and Donald Keene's anthology of modern Japanese literature in English. Her lonely, slightly conceited air piqued his curiosity.

Ben, however, had rarely spoken to any of the foreign students. Being only seventeen, Ben shied away from the banter among the college students and graduate students; all they did was badmouth people anyway. He felt more comfortable with the Japanese students—whom the foreign students dismissed as immature—and found himself keeping company with members of the English Conversation Club, who were always lined up in front of the graffiti wall.

After his Japanese class was over, Ben would stop by the foreign students' lounge. As soon as he got in the door, several Japanese students who'd been standing by the wall would surround him, their eyes focused—like those of nervous hunters readying their aim—yet somehow friendly at the same time. "Hi, Ben," they would say, eagerly launching into English.

The members of the English Conversation Club had fairly decent pronunciation, but the way they carried on a conversation made it unlike any he had ever experienced in English. Instead of a discussion, it was more like an interview—at times an interrogation—as they bombarded him with questions. Apparently, members of the club met beforehand to decide each day's topic of conversation. Some even recited a list of carefully worded questions from a card.

"Do you think Robert Kennedy will become a candidate in the presidential election?"

"Don't you feel guilty about the Vietnam War? What about the dropping of the atomic bomb on Hiroshima?"

"What do you think about the unique spirit of the Japanese people?"

"Are you familiar with the novels of Yasunari Kawabata and Yukio Mishima?"

From the tenor of their questions, he realized that what they really wanted was to subject the West itself to scrutiny. But Ben was fresh out of high school, hardly a politician or an expert on Japan, so he was surprised that they would press him on such difficult issues. Even more unsettling to Ben was the way they listened so attentively to his answers, despite the fact that they were older than he was.

The "Japanese wallflowers," as the foreign students called them, first spoke to Ben two days after classes started. The initial conversation began with "What is your name?"

When he replied, "Ben Isaac," the student who had approached him turned to another student and whispered something in Japanese. Then, after prefacing his question with "Excuse me," he asked in the most elegant Queen's English, "What is your ethnic background?"

"I'm half Polish, half Jewish."

"*Jewwwisssh?*" the student responded, eyes widening, as though he hadn't heard the part about "half" or "Polish." The hunter had bagged a rare breed of animal, and he could hardly contain his excitement. "Well then, what do you think of Zionism?" he asked.

"I don't." Ben had never really given it any thought.

"But surely you support Israel?"

"I don't really care."

"But," the student with the Queen's English persisted, "you are Jewish, are you not?"

Ben didn't know what to say. He was thinking back to that silence on the phone when he called his grandmother.

"I'm a Jew who doesn't dream of Israel."

ONE DAY TOWARD THE END OF SEPTEMBER, THE SHOUTING got louder. A raucous crowd of demonstrators marched across campus and took up positions directly beneath the windows of the foreign students' lounge. In helmets color-coded according to the three factions, the demonstrators proceeded to zigzag in columns in the middle of the street. The late afternoon sun bounced off the hundreds of helmets bobbing up and down to the intense rhythm of the chanting.

There was a loud whistle. A high-pitched cry of *Anpō* blared from the megaphones. This was followed by a chorus of *Funsaaai!* To Ben, this sounded like a desperate question-and-answer session. Gradually the cries of the answer drowned out the question.

Funsaaai! . . . Funsaaai! . . . Funsaaai! . . . Destroy! Destroy! Destroy!

By the time the demonstration moved on to the main gate of the university, only echoes of the shouting remained, mere traces of its former fury. But then the distant shouts of the next group of demonstrators rode in on the crisp autumn air. It was an afternoon full of contradictions, promising to tear up the *ancien régime* by the roots and to create a new heaven and earth in its place.

That day, Ben was talking about the Vietnam War to a rapt audience of three members of the English Conversation Club. During the autumn of 1967, more and more people were speaking out against the war, even in America, but for Ben—who was entering college the following year and would be exempt from the draft for five years—the war was nothing more than images displayed on the television screen in his mother's house. The connection between Vietnam and himself was just a vague, blurry, black-and-white anxiety.

The topic the English Conversation Club had chosen for that day was: "The Vietnam War, American Imperialism, and White Supremacy."

"In other words," the leader began, using his best Queen's English, "I daresay that the bombing raids over Vietnam in recent months by U.S. Air Force F-111s filled with napalm bombs, which engulf rural Vietnamese villages in blue flame, are caused by the same psychology that dropped the atomic bombs on Hiroshima"—here, he used the British pronunciation Hiro-SHEE-ma—"and Nagasaki, where hundreds of thousands of Japanese people lived. In other words, I suspect they both derive from white supremacy, which disregards the lives of Orientals. Subsequently, I must ask how you feel about this as a Caucasian."

That was the question Ben was supposed to answer. The sirens of the riot police could be heard coming from the main gate, but the three members of the English Conversation Club were focused solely on Ben.

If you wanted to talk about supremacy, Ben thought, the buildings along Yamashita Park Avenue that he could see from the roof of the consulate were like a landscape of white supremacy. His father's house was a bastion of white supremacy, pompously presiding over the streets of Yokohama. Yet his father had spent his life on the margins of white society. Had his father been in Europe twenty-five years before, he would have been killed just for bearing the Jewish surname Isaac. Furthermore, the lady of the house, Gui-lan, had several relatives who actually were executed for participating in anti-Japanese activities when she was a young girl in Shanghai. What about the lives of Orientals who lived in Shanghai and Nanjing? When Japanese killed Asians, what kind of supremacy was that? Ben wanted to argue, but he let it go. Instead, he simply replied, "I think those two cases are a little different."

A shadow of displeasure stole across the thin smile of the Queen's English student. Deep in thought, as though searching for the right word, the student next to him finally said, "But isn't it immoral?"

"Sure. Both cases are immoral. But if you look at Japanese history—"

In mid-sentence, Ben had suddenly noticed a young man standing idly behind his three inquisitors. It was a Japanese student he had never seen in the foreign students' lounge before. His round face peered out from beneath his crew cut. Unlike the less militant members of the English Conversation Club, he wore a black school uniform on his stocky frame and was carrying a square W University cap. He stood there awkwardly, perhaps because he didn't understand the English he was overhearing. The three club members glanced at him suspiciously.

"I'm sorry, but where are you from?" the young man said in Japanese, earnestly, if a bit nervously, and loudly. His enunciation, combined with his intonation—which sounded nothing like the Tokyo speech Ben was used to hearing—sent shockwaves through the foreign students' lounge.

"America," Ben replied, turning his attention to the young man.

This did not please the three English Conversation Club members, who had been trying to ignore the intruder. In shaky Japanese, Ben continued, "And you, where are you from?"

Ben meant it as a serious question, but it seemed to catch the young man off guard, rendering him speechless for a moment.

"Aichi Prefecture, Japan." His eyes were crystal clear. Turning away from the club members, who were snickering to each other, he posed another question to Ben: "Why are you speaking English when you're in Japan?"

All of a sudden, the lounge fell silent. The girls sitting on the sofa looked up at the same time.

One of the English Conversation Club members waved his hands dismissively, as if to say, "Don't answer him, just don't bother." The intruder's question, however, was one Ben had asked himself a number of times ever since he had begun commuting between the consulate and the International Studies Center. Outside of Japanese class, where they force-fed him such formalities as *Watakushi wa Beikokujin de gozaimasu* (I am a citizen of the United States), everyone he met spoke nothing but English to him. If he tried speaking to them in Japanese, they would look at him as if he were some kind of talking animal. "My, what lovely Japanese you speak," they would comment, flashing that famous "Japanese smile." Then they would either respond in English or not respond at all. Why? he often wondered. He didn't understand why it had to be that way.

Just as Ben was about to explain this somehow, the club leader pointed at the intruder and let loose a snicker that sounded like the giggles from those female students who pointed at Ben's family during their Sunday walks. "He's quite provincial," he declared, in English as prim as an Oxford professor's.

The young man probably didn't know the English word "provincial," but he knew he was being made fun of. His eyes quickly turned angry. "This may sound rude," he began, then took a breath, looked Ben in the face, and spat out, "but you're just a *kazarimono*."

Pointing with his square cap at the English Conversation Club members, he continued slowly, emphasizing each word. "To these people, you are nothing more than an ornament, an accessory, like a ring or a pendant imported from abroad."

Ben was speechless.

His ears were filled with the echoes of slogans being hurled against the sky by the faraway demonstrators.

Ben felt as though someone had hit him with a wooden sword.

Never short on words, the Queen's English student yelled at the intruder in high-pitched Japanese, "What gives you the right to talk to this dumb *gaijin*?"

The words from the boy's thin lips, which were always kissing up to the foreign students, had suddenly turned venomous. Contempt, both for the young man in the school uniform and for Ben, was dripping from them.

Ben was fed up. Fed up with the foreign students who didn't speak Japanese, fed up with the Japanese who only spoke English, and fed up with himself for being caught in the middle. He was trapped in this room of English, a room where the English language was the most powerful currency of all. The more he remembered the words exchanged in this room, the more he hated it. Everything about this room was sickening.

Kazarimono . . .

His head felt heavy from the bluntness of the word.

Like a door slamming shut in his mind, Ben made a decision. "Okay," he replied, with the inexplicable courage of someone who had taken a hit, "speak Japanese with me."

The round face of the young man registered surprise, which soon became a smile. But it was a genuine smile, not the smug smile of someone relishing his victory.

"Ahl teach ya."

Unable to understand, Ben stared at him blankly.

"I'll teach you."

Ben still didn't understand. The words *ora* and *ore* the young man had used for "I" were not in Ben's Japanese-language textbook.

The late afternoon sunlight fell across the graffiti wall in the foreign students' lounge, flickering above the heads of the English Conversation Club members, who had retreated to their usual spot in front of the wall.

The young man in uniform stared quizzically at Ben's mute face. Suddenly it hit him. "Oh, I see," he mumbled. Then he calmly repeated to Ben, "I . . . will . . . teach . . . you."

As they walked out into the hallway, the young man put on his square cap and introduced himself to Ben. "I am Andō Yoshiharu."

4

Starting the next day, Ben stopped showing up at the foreign students' lounge. As soon as class ended, he left the International Studies Center, skirted the daily gathering of a group that called itself the Middle Core Faction near the bronze statue of the university's founder, and headed out the side gate to an intersection. Andō had shown him the circuitous way from the intersection to his boardinghouse, but it took Ben three times before he finally knew it by heart.

At the top of the hill, on a windswept corner, stood a billboard with apartment listings from the student co-op. Its splashy numbers often caught Ben's eye:

4.5 MATS: ¥6,000
FEE: 2X / DEPOSIT: 2X

Plastered with red flyers written in bold black strokes, the billboard seemed to advertise the legions of young men who had crammed into the city with innumerable dreams and desires. On that early October afternoon, Ben could feel the warm, inviting light of the endless array of four-and-a-half–mat rooms across Tokyo.

When that light flickered on in Ben's heart, he was reminded of his loneliness, trapped in that palatial bedroom in the consulate, surrounded by the banks and trading companies along Yamashita Park Avenue. How he hated those Venetian blinds that dripped extraterritoriality and those cold marble floors that called up Victorian-era missionaries and tradesmen.

Ben stood alone in the crowd busily making their way through the intersection. A falling leaf brushed against his cheek. Laughter tumbled down the stairs from the mahjong parlor above the student co-op, followed by a stream of students in square caps. Ben watched as they lingered, chatting at the corner, then headed off along the tree-lined avenue toward the train station.

Ben turned left, bucking the tide of high school students pouring out an iron gate. After he passed them, their voices bounced back at him: *harro, harro.* They sounded like a gaggle of young geese honking.

As the honking grew fainter, Ben crossed the avenue and escaped into an alley.

On either side stretched a long line of windows of cheap wooden apartment buildings. Some were already lit from within, even though it was only four in the afternoon. The farther he walked, the narrower the sky between the roofs, the patches of blue turning to slivers of gray. . . .

At the end of the innermost narrow alley, a large persimmon tree rising above a wall marked the entrance to Andō's boardinghouse.

Ben took the small path beside the white walls of the newly built house where the landlord lived, quietly following the stepping-stones through the weeds, until he reached the backyard, where the dilapidated boardinghouse emerged from the shadows.

When he set foot in the entryway, which was dark even during the day, the smell from a musty old toilet hit him. One step up from the entrance, on the right, was an old washbasin. In the cracked mirror hanging perilously above it, Ben caught a reflection of his own face. It was a pale face that peered back at him, with curiosity and hesitation written all over it, like an old man's wrinkles.

Down the hall was a wall covered with yellowing newspapers, perhaps to conceal the cracks. Under his fingers, the faded headlines crunched like autumn leaves, the news no longer new. Ben could only read the words テロ (terrorism) and ベトナム (Vietnam). Running his fingers over page after page as though they were Braille, he slowly climbed the unlit stairs to the second floor. From the far end of a long hallway came the soft notes of a flute, which struck him as incongruous.

When he knocked on the door, the sounds of the flute abruptly stopped.

"Oh, hey."

Andō always greeted Ben that way. His invigorating voice echoed through the early evening chill in the room.

Before he knew it, Ben had begun responding with "Hey." Each time he said it, he couldn't help smiling. That's because he kept remembering the dialogue from the chapter on "Meeting Someone for the First Time" in his Japanese-language textbook: *Sumisu to mōshimasu ga, Tanaka-san de irasshaimasu deshō ka.* Excuse me, but my name is Smith. I wonder if you might be Tanaka-*san? Aa Sumisu-san, yōkoso irasshaimashita.* Ah, Smith-*san,* how nice of you to come.

The Japan described in Ben's textbook was worlds away from the reality that confronted his eyes and ears as he stood before this open door at the end of this long, dark hallway.

"Well, don't just stand there."

When he entered Andō's room, the first thing he noticed was a small desk against the far wall. Books and magazines were strewn on the desk. Manga with easy names like *Garo* in *katakana* were interspersed with academic books by people with names Ben couldn't read. One magazine had a Maserati sports car on the cover, and toward the back a double-page spread of a white girl offering her triple-C breasts to the reader. A bamboo fencing sword leaned against the gray wall, where a black school uniform hung below a maroon W University pennant and a photograph of Andō's favorite author posing in military dress. These things lent a vaguely heroic air to the room.

Each of the objects in Andō's room gave the impression of strength and stability amid confusion. They made Ben feel as though he had stepped into a still-life painting by accident. He was always amazed that someone as big and brawny as Andō could survive in such a small painting where he had to move around so delicately.

It's so different, Ben thought every time he came by. Andō's room—and Andō's world, which began in that room and radiated out toward the alleys and slopes around W University like light from a lighthouse—were so different from the "Japan" he had read about in books.

Ben routinely made his way to Andō's room after class. With Andō as his guide, he began exploring that new world. For his part, Andō seemed to take great pleasure in showing his world to Ben.

Andō, who had just come to Tokyo the previous April to study at W University, did all his guiding of Ben in Japanese. He couldn't speak English to save his life. Furthermore, unlike those Japanese students who hovered around the foreign students, he had absolutely no interest in learning English per se. For Andō, English was nothing more than a subject on the college entrance exams. Now that he was safely into college, Andō often boasted, "I'm proud o' bein' Japanese, so why should I hafta speak English?" He also said that since Ben was in Japan, he should speak Japanese. Mimicking Andō's tone of voice, Ben replied, "Obviously." Still, he had never heard such an opinion voiced in the Yokohama consulate or in the International Studies Center, which formed the two pillars of his "Japan."

In the beginning, Ben could comprehend only 10 or 20 percent of what Andō was saying. Andō, though, didn't seem to care if Ben understood or not. "You'll get the hang of it before long," he assured him. He would speak to Ben in the same tone of voice and at the same speed he spoke to Japanese, only with a lot more borrowed words from English mixed in. From the torrent of Japanese words that poured out of Andō's mouth as they walked the streets around the university, Ben managed to pick out a few he knew. By stringing them together in his mind, he tried to figure out what Andō was saying.

Like an older brother taking his deaf-mute younger brother out for a walk, the nineteen-year-old Andō did his best to ignore the seventeen-year-old Ben's handicap, chatting quite normally with him as he walked one step ahead.

Wandering the streets of Tokyo with a Japanese person for the first time in his life, Ben was fascinated by what he saw. He was perpetually confused, unsure where he was. As they navigated those mazelike backstreets, the sky would suddenly appear above them. Out of nowhere Ben would see crowds hurrying across the tree-lined avenue—the swarms of schoolboy uniforms, just like Andō's, and the throngs of female students in lavender and checkered dresses like islands in a sea of black. Above them, a steady stream of slate-colored clouds flowed northward against a dark blue background.

Andō's world stretched as far as the eye could see, along either side of the wide avenue, with its panoramic view of the sky that seemed to refute the myth that Japan was small. His world ran from the Toden streetcar stop, from which a truncated train departed for places with names like KAN-DA and KU-DAN, to the point where the avenue climbed a hill and disappeared around a corner on the way to TA-KA-DA-NO-BA-BA.

For Ben, it was a world of *hiragana*, a world confined to sounds. When he told Andō that this world filled him with a "sense of mystery," Andō just laughed, but the sounds of place names he learned from Andō's mouth that October were the most extravagant things he had ever heard. Still meaningless to him, they were filled with magical possibilities. For people who lived in the city and were used to reading them, those place names evoked images of train stations, banks, brothels, and shopping districts. For Ben, who lived in a world of sounds and syllables, they had a touch of elegance, of mystery, and even, at times, of humor. KAN-DA, KU-DAN, TA-KA-DA-NO-BA-BA—there was a ring to them, like the jangle of keys that could unlock the secrets of the city. At their center was the spot Andō referred to as "the intersection near my place."

From the intersection, heading toward the main gate of the university, on the right side of the street, was a bookstore, where Andō often went to peruse books on literature and music. The first time he took Ben there, Andō pointed to the new releases lined up at the register and pronounced the authors' names, which were all in *kanji*, in a voice loud enough to make the other patrons turn their heads: "This is YO-SHI-MO-TO RYŪ-MEI, this is HA-NI GO-RŌ, this is MI-SHI-MA YU-KI-O. You know him, right?"

From the intersection, heading toward the station, on the corner near the top of the hill, was a *pachinko* parlor. Inside, they would thread their way through the smoke from Peace and Hi-Lite cigarettes, through the throaty, mournful Japanese ballads playing on the public address system, and through the black-on-black rows of students and office workers lined up in front of the machines like the faithful at an altar. "Try this one, Ben," Andō would say, choosing a machine for him. Before long, Andō had taught him what to look for in a machine—the position of the pins at the top—and where to go (two doors down from the Korean barbeque in the alley) to exchange his winnings of Ajinomoto MSG and Meiji chocolate for cash.

Again, from the intersection, in the opposite direction of the *pachinko* parlor, halfway up the avenue and down a lane to the left, was a public bathhouse, where Andō went for his baths and Ben sometimes accompanied him. The bathhouse towered above the lane like some strange temple. They'd duck through the door, slip out of their shoes, and each pay the lady at the counter thirty-seven yen, although it was Andō who'd hand over the money.

On Ben's first visit to the bathhouse, at 4:30 in the afternoon, there were only five or six people in the men's bathing area. A young boy was washing himself alongside his father; when he saw Ben's white body, he tugged his father's hand and pointed. Andō was saying to Ben, in Japanese, "Y'know you wash outside the tub, right?"

After they'd soaped and scrubbed themselves, Ben followed Andō into the large tub, which sat beneath a tile wall clumsily painted to resemble Atami Hot Springs. The water was clear and exceedingly hot. Dipping his foot in, Ben winced. "You don't have to," Andō said, but Ben ignored him. Biting his lip and braving the heat that almost seared the skin off his body, he slowly lowered himself in up to his neck, just like Andō had. Andō watched, bemused, as Ben then leaned his head against the shocking blue of the sea undulating beneath Atami Hot Springs.

"Had enough?" Andō asked. Emerging from the bath, the two young men made their way back to the changing room. As Ben slid the glass door shut and stepped up onto the wooden planks, the light seemed to catch Andō's muscular body at an angle that made it glisten like ancient ivory. Drying off before a mirror, Ben couldn't help but compare his own pale, meager torso to Andō's firm, beautiful body, which seemed to capture the essence of Greek sculpture. In Andō's lean shoulders, chest, and legs, Ben saw the body of a man who had been steeped in a single culture since birth. Andō must have weighed fifty pounds more than he did. Noticing Ben's comparing their bodies in the mirror, Andō remarked, "Ben, you look more Oriental than I do." His laughter filled the room.

Before long, the sky above the intersection took on a bronze patina, like the Bizen ware in his father's study. The late-autumn season Andō called BAN-SHŪ had arrived. Looking up at that BAN-SHŪ sky, which enveloped the intersections and slopes of Tokyo, Ben understood for the first time the beauty of gray. He wanted to tell this to Andō but didn't have the words for it, so, as with many of his discoveries at that time, he had no other choice but to keep it to himself.

On one cold day, the two young men turned right at the intersection and followed the long wall of the high school to a café. Sitting in chairs so tiny that Ben thought they were for children, they warmed their feet before a kerosene heater. Listening to pop songs by the Tigers and the Carnabeats, Andō thumbed through magazines while Ben flipped through his *hiragana* flashcards. On one side of the flashcards was a single *hiragana* syllable and three words using that syllable; on the other side were the romanized pronunciations and the meaning of the words in English. Ben went through his flashcards, reading out loud NA, NA-KA, NA-TSU, NA-MA-E, and writing the *hiragana* in his notebook. Four Japanese students immersed in their English textbooks at the next table dropped what they were doing and stared.

Practicing *hiragana* made Ben think about when he had first become aware of something called Japanese. He was eight or nine and living in Taichung, Taiwan. One day he discovered an old book the former owner of the house had left behind in an alcove. Stuck among the dense clusters of Chinese characters was a squiggly, asymmetrical foreign object—the *hiragana* の. Taking the dust-covered book to his father, Ben asked what the symbol was. His father replied, "That? That's Japanese." He didn't seem particularly pleased by what Ben had dug up.

That? That's Japanese. Now, sitting in a café in Tokyo and studying Japanese, Ben heard his father's words again. Behind the contempt they expressed, his father must have seen the *hiragana* の—which Ben now knew was pronounced "no"—to be something suspicious and womanly, unlike Chinese characters, which represented the world of reason. That *hiragana*, his father no doubt thought, was the mark of a culture that cared nothing for the symmetry of reason and succumbed only to the senses; one would be far better off studying Chinese. Ben remembered nothing else about the conversation with his father that day. All he remembered was quietly leaving his father's bedroom and going to the veranda with the book in his hands. He remembered hearing the carp breaking the surface of the pond as he sat, filled with a sense of wonder as his eyes moved across the yellowed pages from top to bottom and right to left, following the *hiragana* shaped like butterflies flitting through a forest of Chinese characters: の and は and む and ゑ.

Misora Hibari singing "Blood-Red Sun" came on over the speakers as Ben flipped to the flashcard for ぬ. He could write な and に fairly well, but no matter how many times he tried ぬ it never came out the way it looked on the card. When he asked Andō about it, Andō put down his magazine, took Ben's hand, and drew ぬ with his index finger onto Ben's rosy palm. He repeated the complicated strokes three or four times.

This seemed to amuse the students at the next table, and one whispered something in English, which Ben couldn't catch. In the tiny café, the four students erupted into laughter.

Ben pulled his hand back and asked, "What did he say?"

Not knowing what to do, Andō blushed and stayed quiet.

"What did he say . . . about me . . . just now . . . that guy?" Ben asked in choppy Japanese.

Trying not to smile, Andō put his hand to his mouth and then mumbled, "Helen Keller."

ON DAYS THEY DIDN'T GO TO THE CAFÉ, THE TWO young men turned left at the intersection, cut across a courtyard where the walls of the university building were defaced with slogans in bright red paint, then went down into the basement student cafeteria. Andō always chose what to eat. "Hashed beef on rice okay with you today?" he would ask. "Sure," Ben would answer, nodding almost unconsciously. Following Andō's lead, he'd pay sixty yen at the ticket counter. A short time later, he got back a large plate piled with an unfamiliar brown substance, neither solid nor liquid. When they were done eating, Andō smoked a cigarette—his brand was Wakaba. Around that time, Ben began smoking Wakabas too.

Coming up from the basement cafeteria one afternoon, Ben and Andō happened upon a demonstration in the courtyard. Thirty students in white helmets were standing around a bonfire, watching the flames devour the slogans scrawled on billboards. A thin trail of smoke drifted up into the perfect square of sky, framed by the surrounding buildings, and disappeared into the oncoming dusk. As Andō and Ben approached, they were noticed by two or three of the demonstrators at the edge of the group, who turned and stared, surprised, their eyes peering out above the masks covering their noses and mouths.

Andō signaled for Ben to stop when they got about ten feet from the group.

Suddenly, one of the demonstrators began singing—or, rather, screaming—at the top of his lungs, "Arise!" The other demonstrators quickly joined in.

> Arise! you tired and hungry souls,
> The day is growing nearer.

Ben couldn't understand the words, but from the tension in the air and the energy of the chorus, he sensed that something momentous hinged upon that song. Rather than anger, the expression of the demonstrators who huddled in the cold and raised their voices in song seemed closer to ecstasy. The meaningless string of sounds bounced off the four walls of the courtyard.

> Awaken, my fellow countrymen,
> A new dawn is upon us.

Ben was enthralled by the scene—the bonfire, the song, the burning commitment in the dark eyes of the demonstrators.

"Let's get outta here," Andō said, tugging on Ben's sleeve.

When they reached the tree-lined avenue, Andō said, "That was the All-Japan Federation of Students' Self-Governing Associations." To Ben, Andō's explanation, like the chorus of voices far behind them, meant nothing at all. It was only syllables: ZEN-GA-KU-REN.

Ben stared blankly at Andō, who muttered, "Screw 'em," then walked off under the barren limbs stretching between the trees in a direction they hadn't traveled before. Even as he pursued him, Ben could feel the chasm between Andō's world and his own. Andō was fully alive within the Japanese language. But when Andō's words communicated nothing but the sounds of Japanese, Ben felt like he was running beside a river, desperately trying to keep up with the current.

Andō walked on in silence along the avenue, never breaking his stride, not slowing down for Ben. Afraid of losing sight of Andō's black uniform in the oncoming darkness, Ben quickened his pace, wondering where on earth Andō was headed. Suddenly, he was seized by the fear of getting lost in a foreign city at night.

Andō stopped behind a gymnasium built at the foot of a bluff overlooking the campus. When he turned around, his face showed no sign of impatience.

"Ben, listen."

From inside the gymnasium, they could hear the Japanese fencing club shouting high-pitched commands over a din of bamboo swords cracking against one another. Andō pointed to a narrow asphalt path that branched off from the avenue.

"See this?" he asked. "It's a shortcut to Shinjuku."

His voice sounded like he was disclosing an important secret or, rather, a divine revelation.

Choked by weeds on either side, the narrow path meandered up the hill behind the gymnasium toward the dozen apartment buildings standing atop the bluff.

"One of these days, I'll take ya to Shinjuku."

When Andō uttered the name SHIN-JU-KU, Ben thought he heard a quiver in his voice, one that hadn't been there when he taught him all those other place names. Seventeen-year-old Ben sensed something in that quiver that suggested SHIN-JU-KU probably held an inexplicable attraction for nineteen-year-old Andō as well.

The hundreds of windows in the apartment complex atop the bluff reflected the last light of the day. Or perhaps it was the light from SHIN-JU-KU, which burned brightly on the other side of the hill, just out of sight.

A thought floated up in Ben's mind, a memory still fresh from the morning. He was riding the train, on his way to school. He was among the crowds of Tokyo, wrapped in the smells of perfume, pomade, and sweat. His face pressed up against the window, Ben peered out as the train slowed down. Signs of the next station passed one after the other, their white *hiragana* trailing across a navy-blue background. Each sign called out to Ben seductively:

SHIN-JU-KU . . .

SHIN-JU-KU . . .

SHIN-JU-KU . . .

SHIN-JU-KU . . .

SHIN-JU-KU . . .

Soon the doors opened, and the crowds were sucked out. Left inside the car, Ben felt a strong desire wash over him. He wanted to get off the train with those people. He wanted to blend in with the crowds and follow in their footsteps.

SHIN-JU-KU . . . The word itself produced a warm feeling of gray, of the city, of Japan, of late autumn. Realizing he could never fit into that crowd, Ben was filled with a foreboding emptiness, a kind of feeling he had never known before. The feeling lingered for a brief moment before it was quickly swallowed up in the crowd that got on the train.

Still, in that brief interlude, which had now become a memory, Ben discovered a source of pleasure. Looking straight at Andō's face, he exclaimed, "I know SHIN-JU-KU too."

Andō simply smiled. It was an indefinable smile, which seemed to say, "'Course ya do."

Ben felt a quiet surge of emotion. Andō—like a selfless teacher who derives satisfaction from showing a student new places and teaching him new things—had brought him all the way to this corner of the city and shown him this narrow asphalt path half covered with weeds. And his sole purpose was to share the most precious piece of knowledge he possessed.

That's when it happened. As he studied Andō's face, Ben had an epiphany.

Helen Keller must have experienced the same kind of emotion that I'm feeling now, he thought.

She couldn't see anything, she couldn't hear anything, she didn't know anything, and she couldn't know anything. The deaf-mute little girl who lived in darkness was essentially a *gaijin*, an outsider to the people around her and even to her own family.

When her generous, brilliant teacher wrote the letters W-A-T-E-R on the palm of her hand, she suddenly understood this to mean the cold water flowing over her skin. In that instant, by *knowing* water, Helen must have been shocked by the realization that she was part of the world for the first time, that she really *existed*.

Andō's smiling round face sent a clear message: "'Course ya do, 'course ya know it."

The ridge rising behind Andō was now outlined by the glare of SHIN-JU-KU, which had begun to shine like the light from a distant festival.

This Japanese city greeted outsiders with the absolute conviction that *they didn't know anything and they couldn't know anything*. Now, for the first time since entering this city, Ben knew one thing for sure.

I know SHIN-JU-KU too.

Like a thirst at last quenched, a simple pleasure permeated Ben's body.

He had a premonition: unlike Helen, he could hear sounds loud and clear, and someday he would be able to solve the mystery of this country's sounds and then be allowed to participate in it.

At a police box that faced stone steps leading up to a shrine, Ben and Andō parted. The tree-lined avenue headed uphill from there. For Ben, who had to make it home before nightfall, it was near time to say good-bye to Japan for the day. Mingling with the crowds, he headed up the avenue toward the train station. Like a vagrant picking up the cigarette butts and five-yen coins on the sidewalk, Ben walked along scavenging bits and pieces of language spewed out by passersby. Then, with this meager stash of Japanese tucked away in his heart, he returned to that marble world in Yokohama, which was both a part of Japan and apart from it. Late at night, in his bedroom on the second floor of the consulate, he went through his pickings as though appraising precious old coins salvaged from a lost empire. One by one, he turned the words over in his mind, trying to memorize their shape and sound.

5

THROUGH THE PICTURE WINDOW OVER HIS FATHER'S shoulder, Ben could see the funnels of the passenger liners docked on the south pier, jutting out beyond the leafless trees in the park. In the twilight, the large eagles emblazoned on the funnels of the SS *President Wilson* seemed to glare at the hammer and sickle emblazoned on the funnel of the MS *Khabarovsk* at the adjacent dock.

On the long oak table in the formal dining room were four silver pots of dumplings, their skins milky white in broth under the soft light of the chandelier. Ben sat on one of the hard oak chairs, gazing out at the harbor scene. Each time a cargo ship near the breakwater blew its horn, Jeffrey, who was seated across from Ben, started bouncing up and down. Turning to Gui-lan, who was at the far end of the table, Jeffrey squealed, in Chinese, "The ship farted!"

"Shh!" his mother replied.

"Mommy, the ship farted!" Jeffrey screamed louder.

Unable to keep from laughing, Gui-lan looked to Ben's father at the head of the table for help.

"That's enough," he said in a stern voice.

Jeffrey clammed up.

Aside from Jeffrey's outbursts, dinner at the consular residence was a quiet affair. On nights when there were no guests or when their Japanese chef was not used, Gui-lan would prepare dumplings and meat buns herself. The four family members would eat in silence, sitting far from each other at a table that normally seated sixteen. At receptions and garden parties, Ben's father was famous for his sardonic wit, which the WASPs at the embassy referred to as "Brooklyn humor," but with the family he was a man of few words, exchanging only a handful of Shanghainese phrases with Gui-lan during dinner.

In November, as Ben started coming home from Tokyo later and later, his father became noticeably colder toward him. On one occasion, his father picked up a State Department report entitled "Vietnam: Victory This Year" and, ignoring the entire family, buried his nose in it with a look of irritation.

There were reasons for his irritation besides Ben's increasing tardiness. He wasn't pleased with the way Ben shut himself up in his room after dinner. And he didn't like it when Ben changed the radio station from the Far East Network to a local broadcaster that played Japanese pop songs and ballads and made jokes no one in the Isaac household could comprehend. He'd be going through documents in his study next door, hear the gibberish, and knock on the door telling Ben to turn it off. He'd find Ben hunched over his desk—face strained and pale in profile—frantically filling notebooks with *hiragana*, *katakana*, and clumsy *kanji*. On the edge of the desk would be two dog-eared translations of Japanese novels: *Kokoro* and *The Temple of the Golden Pavilion*.

One night, his father opened the door to his bedroom and, seeing Ben again at his desk, muttered, "You look like one of those Jap monks copying sutras at a temple."

Ben didn't flinch.

His father spoke louder this time, aiming his words at Ben's skinny back: "You really think you can become Japanese by doing that?"

Ben kept his mouth shut and continued to write the characters from top to bottom in steady strokes. A shudder ran down his back.

"For all that studying you've been doing in Tokyo, you still don't know the first thing about Japan."

Ben was shocked by his father's persistence, considering how reticent he usually was.

"No matter how much you learn to speak *their* language, in *their* eyes you'll always be like me: a dumb *gaijin* who can't speak properly and never wanted to. Even if you go the plaza in front of the Imperial Palace and scream 'Long live the Emperor!' in perfect Japanese and slit your stomach open, you'll never be one of *them*." His words hanging in the air, his father softly shut the door.

Ben's tardiness only got worse. Loath to leave Tokyo until the last rays of the sun had left the sky above the intersection near Andō's place, he sometimes didn't get off the Yamashita Park Avenue bus before the streetlights had already come on. By the time he showed up in the dining room one evening, the family had almost finished eating. At the head of the table, his father slowly raised his eyes to meet Ben's.

"If you hate it here so much, I'll send you home."

When his father said "home," Ben's first thought was of Andō's world. Just an hour ago, he had been walking around in that world. But when he looked into his father's face, he realized that "home" for Ben meant America to his father. Ben said nothing, fixing his gaze on the view through the picture window over his father's shoulder, searching for something to grasp on to among the blinking harbor lights.

From the park to the breakwater in the distance, the harbor was full of foreign ships. American ships, Russian ships, ships from other countries. Andō had once said to him: "I bet you can see tons of GA-I-KO-KU-SEN from your old man's place." And now, that was what he was doing: seeing all those GA-I-KO-KU-SEN, foreign ships, in Japanese, without even realizing it. Outside-country-ships. Alien ships. Ships that brought people to Japan from the outside, people who were *alien*, people like his father. The black ships, trading ships, and warships that had brought barbarians—*ketō*—of every kind and color: Dutch, Portuguese, Americans, red-haired goblins and blue-eyed devils, blacks and Jews. And me. And me . . . no, *ore*, he thought, switching into Japanese. I—*ore*—may have come here on a ship like all the others, but I—*ore*—am totally different from them! Unsure whom to address this to or which language to translate it into, Ben felt his appeal catch in his throat. Framed by the picture window, his father's big, blue-gray eyes shone with anticipation, waiting for an apology that would never come.

Ben averted his eyes—the same color as his father's—and dipped his chopsticks into one of the silver pots.

When it became clear that Ben was not going to respond, his father clammed up himself. Ben stuffed the remaining dumplings into his mouth. An oppressive silence settled over the dining room, more so than usual. Like gray gobbled up by black, the outlines of the trees in the park were swallowed up by the night sky, while the lights on the cargo ships and the warehouses on the piers became even more vibrant.

Gui-lan got up to clear the silver pots from the table. All of a sudden, a high-pitched screech—something between a woman's scream and a car's brakes—came from the direction of Yamashita Park Avenue, piercing the thick glass of the picture window and tearing through the dining room.

"Lights out!" his father yelled, jumping up from his chair.

They all ran around switching off the dining room chandelier, the hall lights, the table lamps in the parlor. . . . In the darkness, the family peered out the parlor window. The Stars and Stripes fluttered in the floodlights shining from the four corners of the front yard. Beyond the fence, on the far side of the avenue, a hundred or so people were gathered. Someone in the front row yelled into a megaphone:

Yankii . . .

A chorus of solemn voices responded:

Gō hōmu.

U.S. Marines and Japanese policemen stood on guard in front of the consulate. Like rumblings underground, the cries of the demonstrators reverberated deeply through the pavement.

Yankii . . . *Gō hōmu.*

"They sound pretty weak, honey," Gui-lan whispered into Ben's father's ear.

"Well, that's the Yoyogi faction for you," his father muttered, his face pressed up against the glass and his eyes squinting in the dark.

Ben didn't understand the difference between the Yoyogi faction and the anti-Yoyogi faction, but he didn't spot any helmets, masks, or clubs in the crowd of demonstrators. Whatever faction they belonged to, they were nothing like those students who sang so resolutely in the courtyard of the university. There were adults in this group—perhaps it was a labor union?—including a middle-aged man with a crimson headband who was as bald as Ben's father. The group was serious but lacked enthusiasm, making it more depressing than menacing.

The low-pitched chorus hurled at the consulate every few seconds echoed off the walls of the darkened parlor:

Gō hōmu.

The words literally got lost in translation: *kuni ni kaere* (go back to your country), *ie ni kaere* (go back to your house), *kokyō ni kaere* (go back to your hometown). As he looked across Yamashita Park Avenue, Ben understood how this simple slogan, which he had heard in countless port towns across Asia, was perhaps the cruelest joke they could play on Americans in Asia.

The Europeans, who occasionally came to dinner parties at the consulate, were immune to such mockery. The French and Italians would shrug it off with a laugh: "Oh, we'll go home soon enough. *Ciao, au revoir, sayonara.*" The Americans, however, had abandoned their homes or had been driven from them. That's what made them Americans. For them, especially those who sought refuge in towns across Asia after they had found America too much to bear, to "go home" meant retracing the path of their escape. It meant retracing every step of the way by which they had run off in the night, leaving their homes behind, clutching the family heirlooms. For the four individuals bearing the surname Isaac huddled here at the window of the consulate, the taunts of "go home" stung. Where on earth was home? Brooklyn? Shanghai? Or some distant, dreamy Jerusalem?

Where was Ben's home? Since he was a kid, he'd been dragged to a string of so-called homes: his parents' houses in Asia, his mother's house in Virginia, and now his father's house, from which he might get sent "home." He shifted his gaze from the demonstrators to his father, his stepmother, and his half-brother, who were staring down at the crowd from the darkness. They looked more like a band of refugees than a family. They were Yankees without a home to "go home" to.

After a signal from the leader of the group, the demonstrators, who had been shaking their fists and shouting, immediately stopped, and with the speed of a clean-up crew at an official function, they rolled up their red flags and banners and loaded them, along with their megaphones, onto a light truck. Then they picked up and left without another peep. The Japanese policemen who had been standing in front of the consulate hopped into their patrol cars and sped off. The marines drew back inside the fence. Silence quickly returned to Yamashita Park Avenue. The Japanese who had been protesting at the consulate, and those who had been protecting it, had all returned to their respective homes.

Other than Andō's room, Ben had not been in any Japanese home. In the brief interval until the table lamps and the chandeliers in the consulate were turned back on, however, he imagined he knew every inch of the places everyone had gone home to. The two-story mortar houses jammed along the sides of the canal that poured into the harbor. The brightly lit housing developments past the warehouses, the factories, and the shopping districts. The small wooden structures clinging to the foot of the Yamate Bluff, where the Foreigners' Cemetery was. Their homes—with glazed windowpanes shutting out strangers from the happy families behind them—were a clear image in his mind. As he now gazed at the wide, deserted sidewalk under the streetlights along Yamashita Park Avenue, Ben felt intensely envious of all *those people*.

When the lights came on, Ben went straight to his room. Scraps of paper with characters scrawled vertically were strewn about his desk. The Venetian blinds were still raised in the window beside it. The Stars and Stripes, in the glare of floodlights, was waving, blocking any view.

Somehow this brought to mind another November night when the Stars and Stripes was caught in a similar glare of floodlights. Ben was living with his mother in Virginia, and he had joined a procession of people marching up a hill. Halfway up the hillside, the freshly dug grave of the assassinated president was awash with light. It was 1963, four years ago. Ben was thirteen. In every house along the two-mile walk back from Arlington National Cemetery to his mother's house, televisions broadcasted the events of the day. Ben turned on the giant television in his house too. The blinding light from those floodlights filled every channel until the dead of night.

The Stars and Stripes began to flap loudly, like a sail rippling in the wind. Turning away from the window, Ben gathered up the scraps of paper covered with Japanese. He dreamed of putting the pieces of the language together, of being reborn in a new tongue and unlocking all its secrets.

His father didn't come to his room to say anything. From beyond his closed door, Ben could hear Jeffrey hollering in a mixture of English and Chinese. After a while, when the young boy's screams died down, he heard his father and Gui-lan's footsteps as they shuffled through the study next door, the sound fading away as they retired to their bedroom in back. The only lights on were in Ben's room and on the stairwell landing.

Had it been summer, it would have been time to climb the marble staircase and go out onto the roof.

Voices in heavily accented English drifted up from the front yard. The Japanese guardsmen were greeting the marines as they changed shifts. The marines, wearing impeccable white gloves, marched in step to the flagpole. They saluted the flag, then slowly lowered it. Seconds before it might have touched the ground, a pair of gloved hands snatched it up, and the two marines then folded the flag neatly. The floodlights were switched off, plunging the front yard into darkness.

At that moment Ben made up his mind to leave his father's house for good.

That night, he would head to Andō's room. He had a hunch where he would go the next day.

Stuffing the three thousand yen left over from his November allowance and the ID card with an eagle stamped above his face into his pocket, Ben walked from his room into his father's study. He cracked open the door from the study to the stairwell landing. The Oriental antiques his father had enshrined on the bookshelves in place of religious icons glimmered in the light.

6

WITHOUT SO MUCH AS LOOKING AT HIM, THE EXPRESSIONLESS old woman took his three ten-yen and two five-yen coins and slid a bottle of warm milk across the counter to him. He gulped it down, the milk surging through his empty stomach with the force of a flash flood. Fighting the urge to vomit, Ben walked out the south exit of Shinjuku Station into the light of morning.

The stretch of sky above the wide overpass was the color of slate, as though someone had draped a heavy coat over the inky dawn landscape.

The railroad tracks, which would have stretched to the edge of the sky, disappeared beneath the roofs and antennas that serrated the horizon. The wind whistled through the darkened, rusty frames of neon signs and garish billboards, now colorless in the dull light.

It was unlike any wind Ben had felt in the city before. It was not a gentle breeze but rather a strong, pure force of nature, which carried an echo of wintry winds blowing down from the northern mountains and scouring withered fields, tearing through the dreary condominium complexes and flashy entertainment districts. It seemed intent on sweeping away the grime that had accumulated overnight while the city slept. At least that's what it conjured for Ben. The cold wind on his hands and neck actually felt refreshing, even pleasant. As he set foot across the overpass, he heard the voice of his father warning him about "places like Shinjuku."

I finally did it, Ben thought, the words floating up in his mind in Japanese: *tōtō orichatta. I finally got off the train with everyone else. Minna to issho ni orichatta.* Ben smiled to himself, like a juvenile delinquent congratulating himself for pulling off a petty crime. He felt a sense of solidarity with these people—or perhaps it was a heightened curiosity. On the overpass he stopped to look around, his long, wispy blond hair flying in the wind. All around him, the masses of SHIN-JU-KU were moving briskly, in a predetermined direction. As they encountered Ben in their path, their flow split to go around him, merged once again downstream, and spilled onto the streets beyond the overpass.

Ben rejoined the flow, continuing to a point on the overpass where the sidewalk branched off into a narrow slope. He followed the lane and came to an enormous old stone monument on a plot of land enclosed by a low, rusting fence. The area was surprisingly quiet. The adjacent alley that ran through a maze of cheap bars and restaurants was deserted at this hour. Farther down, in a switchyard, freight trains were fast asleep on the tracks that wound through the canyons of Tokyo. Everything was wrapped in gray, not a shadow to be seen.

As the clouds began to move ever so slightly, the stone monument seemed to strain against the sky, as if to reassert a forgotten history. Ben sensed something antagonistic, not majestic, about it. On the weathered surface of the dull brown stone, which seemed to bear the dirt of decades, were carved the characters 昭和三年 御大典記念.[2] Ben could read the group of characters on the left, which said "Shōwa 3," which was the year 1928, but he had no idea what the larger five characters on the right meant. All he knew was that this vaguely threatening stone, which reigned over the rooftops and alleyways of SHIN-JU-KU, was a there for a reason. If he couldn't read it, he figured, it had to be a signpost for him.

Looking around, Ben realized he was not alone after all. Under a dead tree with branches stretching toward the monument, two men were reading a newspaper, the headlines in bright red characters.

Dressed in black workmen's uniforms and socks with rubber soles, they were staring at Ben.

Half expecting to hear another *harro*, Ben put on a faint smile, but the two men only glared at him.

Instinctively Ben stepped back from the fence. The men kept their eyes on him. Ben didn't know what to do. He had never encountered such cold-hearted looks before.

To be sure, Ben had some knowledge of racial animosity. After all, Isaac was a Jewish name, and Jews had been vilified for giving birth to Jesus and then killing him. But in America Ben was considered Caucasian. When he was attending a suburban white high school, he went one Saturday night into the city with friends. On a dimly lit street he encountered a down-and-out alcoholic, a black man whose vacant pink eyes looked right into his and conveyed a message: "Go to hell." It was hatred that resembled a kind of conspiracy, a dirty secret understood by both parties, the result of four hundred years of oppression. Ben saw no curiosity, contempt, or fear. On that night in that American city, the first thing his white man's eyes saw in the black man's eyes was a simple, natural desire to kill.

Here in Shinjuku, however, the cold, sharp light Ben saw in those four eyes—two of which were surprisingly clear, he thought—carried a different message. They conveyed wariness, like when something unfamiliar jumps into view. At the same time, they expressed annoyance, like when moviegoers spot a smudge on the screen. He scurried down the slope, feeling their stares on his back.

The men did not look away. Their eyes were like those of the guardian stone dogs at a shrine, keeping watch over those who appear where they don't belong and those who pass by where they're not welcome.

Ben found himself at the top of a steep flight of narrow stone steps. He now heard the men laughing.

Gaijin.

You don't belong here.

The voices were surprisingly high-pitched, like a woman reprimanding a small child.

Ben looked down the steps. Maybe he didn't belong anywhere.

He took a step, his feet almost sliding out from under him. The stairs were slippery, their edges worn away by generations of Shōwa-era feet. *If I'm not careful,* he thought, *I might slip and fall all the way to the bottom. Or I might fall off the smooth face of the earth entirely.* Suddenly, his body felt perilously light. The world seemed to spin around him.

Ben bolted down the steps to the streets of Shinjuku.

THE END OF NOVEMBER

EARLY ONE NOVEMBER MORNING, SOMETIME NEAR THE END of the 1960s, a seventeen-year-old boy wearing a blue jacket ran down a narrow flight of stone steps. When he reached the bottom, he found himself at a small intersection of two streets: one that ran beneath the overpass at the south exit of Shinjuku Station and one that came from the entertainment district and ducked under the overpass. Just as he was catching his breath, a crosswind rippled through his jacket and tousled his wispy blond hair.

The wind was blowing from the direction of the overpass. Beneath it was a line of stalls locked up in chains. The chains were twisting in the wind and clanging against the stalls. The stone wall behind the stalls was plastered with red and black flyers. Old ones had been torn off and new ones put up in their place, like a palimpsest. The flyers were filled with *kanji* he had never seen before. What were they advocating? Fascism? Communism? Ben Isaac had no idea. The only thing he could comprehend was the sound of the wind sighing through the overpass, signifying November. To his eyes, it looked like the wind had picked up a bunch of screams and splattered them against the stone wall.

Turning away, Ben felt around in his pocket for his money—2,700 yen and some loose change—and the ID card with the eagle stamped above his face (the embassy-issued card that his diplomat father jokingly called "your ticket to extraterritoriality"). Once he was sure they were there, he looked back at the steps he had just run down. At the top of the embankment, the stone monument carved with the characters 昭和三年 御大典記念 towered like a smokestack emitting no smoke. Below it, the corrugated tin roofs of bars and restaurants hugged the embankment in a semicircle. Wedged between the steps and the eaves of the tin roofs was an old concrete toilet.

With its two empty windows cut out at eye level, the toilet had the look of a bunker abandoned by a retreating army. On this first foray into SHIN-JU-KU, he felt as if invisible sentries were monitoring him from behind. He even thought he could hear them whispering, "Just for you, you may pass."

Ben stepped out into the street that led to the entertainment district.

Gray November morning

The words came back to him from long ago, their sound echoing in his head.

But in the ten or so hours since he had left his father's house, Ben suddenly realized, English had been erased from his mind.

In the gray November morning air, neon signs were flashing on and off, generating heat. He walked past a *pachinko* parlor named Peace and a pornographic theater named International, through a world of pink, purple, and silvery temptations that were all but illegible to his tired blue-gray eyes. Passing a used bookstore with the manga *Garo* displayed out front, he approached a Chinese restaurant spewing yellow steam from the cracks between its vermilion-lacquered doors. From the side street he had just come down to the intersection up ahead, and from the stairs hidden behind doors made of glass, wood, and iron, snippets of music and conversation flowed together, intermingling on the patchwork of rough-hewn paving stones at his feet. From inside one of the shops, a husky voice belted out a tune—this one he could understand:

My dear, I learned it all from you:
Drinking and smoking, and lying too.

Enraptured, Ben walked on, forgetting the fear he had felt when he charged down the stone steps. Like a gravitational force, the sound of the *hiragana* word SHIN-JU-KU pulled him along the sidewalk. He had no idea where he should turn. Nor did he particularly care. Maybe that was the message of this utterly chaotic jumble of streets: that there was no difference between going straight and turning a corner. When Ben had left his father's house the previous night, he had also turned his back on his future. Now, the morning after, all he had left was the freedom to go where he pleased. He didn't have much money in his pocket, but the topsy-turvy maze was irresistible.

The maze seemed to go on forever. A shiver passed from the soles of his feet through his skinny body.

He was like the wandering Jew or, rather, like a pale mouse trying to find its way in a laboratory labyrinth. In spite of his hunger, he crawled around stupidly, letting his instincts lead the way at each intersection. Without a thought to either reward or punishment, Ben Isaac kept walking, doggedly pursuing the SHIN-JU-KU that always remained one step ahead of him.

WHEN HE TURNED RIGHT, BEN FOUND HIMSELF IN FRONT OF a pub and the entrance to a building next door. He continued on, weaving through piles of black and blue plastic bags of rotting garbage. He kicked at the fallen leaves and pieces of paper with the words 千円 でOK[1] swirling in the wind at his feet. All the while, he moved through the curious gazes of everyone he passed. Ben walked farther, trying to crack the codes of the city that appeared before his eyes: the signs for local bars, the billboards covered with advertisements, and the flyers plastered on every telephone pole shouting four-character slogans like 安保粉砕 and 昭和維新.[2]

Just past the ¥100 Tempura Rice Bowl joint, he ran across a bored-looking guy wearing a white waiter's uniform, standing under a sad-looking willow tree near the door to a café. The two-story café was stuck between two tall buildings, reminding Ben of a stout, stone-faced king flanked by guards. At the entrance, beside a picture window tinted the color of whisky, was a sign that read 凮月堂 and, next to it, the word FUGETSUDO.

When Ben approached, the waiter didn't even look at him. Instead, he reached into his pocket with soiled, slender fingers and took out a crumpled, light-green box of Wakaba cigarettes. "Think I care if you go in?" he seemed to say as he lit up. Offering neither a *harro* nor a "welcome," he just puffed away.

With no hesitation, Ben went in.

He found himself inside a wide, deep room. On either side of a long passageway were round tables in a salon-style arrangement, with several chairs around each table. Under a ceiling as tall as a temple's, Ben proceeded awkwardly toward the back.

There were three wait staff, and no customers besides Ben. The place looked like it had just opened for the day. From the way the employees were standing around in front of a potted palm, they seemed to be waiting for a ceremony to begin. The laziness, the tedium, and the bleariness of eyes unfit for morning that he saw in each of their faces, however, told him that they had served in this ceremony many times before and were sick and tired of it.

Ben looked around the room, at the empty chairs and tables, at the sickly foliage of the plants, and finally at the large wall on the left. From among the various drawings and posters on the wall, a single black-and-white photograph caught his eye.

He walked up to the wall for a better look and immediately recognized the photograph, which he'd seen in either *The Washington Post* or *Time* magazine. It was of a young girl, twelve or thirteen years old, Asian, skinny, surely Vietnamese. She'd been captured by the U.S. military and had been unable to return to her village. A black blindfold covered her eyes, and her mouth was tightly shut. She was a refugee from a modern war, solemnly enduring her pain in a tropical country where there was no November, suffering humiliation at the hands of soldiers and photographers alike. Her haggard face looked down contemptuously upon the peaceful morning in Fugetsudo.

Ben too had spent his childhood years in a tropical country where there was no November. The difference was, he was the son of those doing the capturing.

Ashamed at himself for staring at the photograph, Ben decided to go up to the second-floor balcony. Long and narrow, it resembled a gallery in a European cathedral. Climbing the stairs with the same lightheadedness he had felt when he ran down the stone steps, Ben took a seat where he could see the entire first floor of the café.

The second he sat down, he was hit by a wave of fatigue.

Judging from the odd look that came over the waitress, he realized that he had just ordered a coffee in Japanese. As he double-checked his pocket for his embassy ID and cash, his senses grew dimmer. The next thing he knew, a cup of coffee, a glass of water, and the check were sitting on the table.

After a bit, the sound of a needle dropping onto a record tore through the thin membrane of silence stretched over this mysterious room. It was a harsh sound, like someone hacking a path through the jungle. Then a male chorus began to sing. Ben's ears perked up. It was a Gregorian chant. Dark, undulating waves of Latin swept from one corner of Fugetsudo to the other.

Libera me.

These were the only words Ben could understand from the chant that so unexpectedly broke the silence of the SHIN-JU-KU morning. *Libera me.* Set me free. The song was a cry for help from the spirit of a dead man. Lighting a cigarette, Ben listened as the dead man's chorus got progressively louder, suffusing the interior of the café with the intensity of black ink spreading across a white sheet of paper.

Libera me.

It was a passionate and rhythmical hymn, born from the darkest depths of the human voice. Filtered through the morning light of SHIN-JU-KU, however, it lost the aura of a Catholic church and came to sound like a cry for escape by the living.

Ben closed his eyes. He had hardly slept the previous night. He remembered the night sky above the harbor he used to gaze at from his bedroom in his father's house. On the far horizon, the water merged with the sky and the November firmament simply disappeared into the pitch-black Pacific Ocean. After he'd turned off the Far East Network broadcast and the sound of traffic along Yamashita Park Avenue subsided, he'd lie in bed listening to the waves lapping against the seawall of the park. Like a chant, the sound of the waves rose and fell in a seductive rhythm, luring him to distant shores. . . .

Now, the morning after leaving that house, he had taken shelter in the most unlikely of places. Under the blind gaze and silent curses of a refugee girl, Fugetsudo was like a huge temple. Ben was a lone infidel who had wandered inside. In their lightly soiled uniforms, the waiters and waitresses looked like pale-faced acolytes and nuns devoting themselves to a religious sect in decline, anxiously awaiting the arrival of more believers. What must they be meditating on, he wondered, as they stood around listlessly in the shadows of the potted palm?

AS THE LAST STRAINS OF THE GREGORIAN CHANT FADED away, the music changed to an orchestral piece Ben had never heard before. When he looked out the window at the end of the passageway, he saw that it had gotten darker outside. A light drizzle had begun to fall, its filaments trickling through the strands of the willow tree. The rain was almost inaudible.

A sound caught his attention. Not the rain, not a musical instrument. A groan.

A faint guttural sound, like that of a small animal caught in a trap in the forest.

Ben put out his cigarette. Fixing his eyes on the shadows near the window, he could make out the form of a person leaning against an indistinct table. Half-hidden behind that figure was another person. Two ghostly white faces appeared, both framed by long black hair.

The first person was moaning softly. Reaching a slender arm up from below, the second person was delicately stroking the first person's back. Or were the white fingers moving at all? Ben peered into the dark corner at the end of the passageway. How long had those blurry clumps of white, black, and gray been over there? he wondered.

A voice came out of the shadows.

"Water, please."

It was a young woman's voice.

"Could I have some water, please?"

The same voice. But the second time, she sounded desperate, like she was begging someone for water instead of ordering it.

The waitress working the second floor was nowhere to be found, so Ben decided to take his water over. When he got closer, he saw that the figure leaning motionlessly against the table was a thin man with long hair.

"Here you are," Ben said, taking a step into the shadows.

He could see the troubled expression on the woman's pale face. In hesitant Japanese, Ben said, "I haven't touched it, so please take mine," offering her the glass of water.

The woman stroking the man's back whispered, "Thank you." With her other hand, she took the glass in her waxy fingers and lifted it to the man's pale lips.

The man appeared to be unconscious. His eyes remained shut.

"Don't worry about him," the woman said, glancing up at Ben.

Just then, Ben realized that his own face was hidden in the shadows. She *can't tell*, he thought.

"He's just a little high from too many painkillers. Nothing serious."

Ben didn't understand why it was "nothing serious," but he didn't think it was a good idea to meddle, so he stepped back and returned to his table.

Trying not to think about the man and woman in the shadows, Ben looked down onto the first floor of the café. Five or six customers were now scattered among the tables that had been empty only a moment ago. Here and there, he could see steam from coffee and smoke from cigarettes rise. Like tendrils of smoke from signal fires dotting the plains, they climbed toward the ceiling and vanished.

"Oh . . . you soldier?"

The question flew up from behind him in English. It was a sudden, jarring sound, like when the needle had touched the old record earlier.

When he turned around, the woman from the shadows was standing next to him.

Taken aback, Ben shook his long blond hair and replied, in Japanese, "No, I'm not."

Under the light, the woman's face was like alabaster. She was staring suspiciously at Ben's face. As though his Japanese words had evaporated into thin air, she pressed on in English, "Tourist?"

"No."

"Missionary?"

"No."

"Hippie?"

"No."

Various categories of *gaijin* oozed from the woman's mouth one after another, but he didn't fit into any of them. . . . Her face became angry, as though she had been tricked.

"Well then, what the hell are you?"

In her impatience, the woman had reverted to her mother tongue.

Ben looked over at the opposite wall. After some thought, he replied, "I am a BŌ-MEI-SHA."

"A . . . *refugee*? Wow, you know some pretty big words, don't you? Where are you escaping from?"

Ben's eyes stopped on the pursed lips of the refugee girl.

"From a war."

"A war?" There was an undertone of anger in the woman's voice. "Aren't you guys the ones waging the war?"

Ben wanted to say that he was escaping from "you guys"—who were actually "my guys"—but he couldn't express it very well, so he said nothing.

"You sound like a deserter, with all that stuff about escaping from a war. A deserter came in here once, you know, with people from the Vietnam Peace Alliance."

The woman looked Ben over, from his blond hair to his scuffed-up shoes. A dubious expression came over her face, which was far whiter than Ben's skin. Ben felt like he was being studied by a ghost.

"But you don't seem like a deserter. Aren't you really a tourist or something?"

The image of those crowds walking in droves across the overpass swept through his mind: a flood of *them*, rushing straight ahead with somewhere to go.

In a weak, half-resigned voice that he almost didn't recognize as his own, Ben mumbled, "Yes."

"I knew it," she said. His answer seemed to satisfy her. She smiled faintly. "Still, your Japanese is pretty good."

As Ben was searching for an appropriate way to respond, the man called out from the shadows, "Rika." He sounded a few years older than Ben and the woman. His voice was hoarse, as though his high hadn't worn off yet. The woman quickly shut up and went back to her lover in the shadows.

Conversations and laughter bubbled up from the first floor of the café. Jokes and exclamations Ben couldn't understand floated by the photograph of the refugee girl.

Music returned to Ben's ears. He heard a harpsichord cadenza, followed by a flute solo. The music swelled, as though it were taunting its listeners, ringing out so clearly that Ben thought he could hear each individual note leaving the flute.

The dove design on the box of cigarettes on the table caught his eye. He reached for them, but stopped. Instead, he took his embassy ID card out of his pocket. Then he lit a match and watched his pale face, beneath the stamp of an eagle, go up in flames.

ON NOVEMBER NIGHTS IN THE EARLY SIXTIES, BEN AND his mother often sat in the parlor of her Virginia house and watched television together. With their backs to the window, where the Virginia night sky through the lace curtains seemed almost white, his mother would sit in the armchair while Ben took the sofa beside it. The parlor was just off the whitewashed porch, and against the wall stood a tall teak bookcase. Its shelves were lined with various mementoes of the Orient—yellowed *netsuke*, a Kutani-ware platter, a plump Buddha from Taiwan—that his mother had brought back to America after leaving his father. Sitting on a lace mat below was a nineteen-inch, black-and-white television set. It was a 1962 Westinghouse, he seemed to recall.

Before its arrival, Ben had never seen a television before. The day after it was delivered, he got up early in the morning and snuck into the living room from his bedroom on the first floor. By the light of the moon reflecting off the white columns on the porch, he turned the dial to ON.

Nothing came on. The nineteen-inch screen was pitch black. When he tried turning the channel dial, a large "5" appeared.

He turned the dial again. Gray waves filled the screen, undulating like the surface of a dark ocean, along with the grating sound of static. So as not to wake his mother, who was asleep in her second-floor bedroom, Ben turned the volume almost to OFF and crouched down before the television, transfixed by the rolling waves on the screen. Recalling the bright blue of the tropical straits he had seen from his father's jeep, he tried to conjure up the gray Atlantic Ocean, which he had never seen. It was supposedly only a three-hour drive away, even in his mother's 1956 Chevrolet. For Ben, who had returned home to an America he had never seen before, the proximity of the Atlantic Ocean was almost as unbelievable as the existence of November.

After his mother got home from her waitress job, Ben would have dinner with her in their tiny kitchen. Then they would go into the parlor and watch the *CBS Evening News* and *The Lucy Show*. Her expression was always the same, whether she was watching the news about the Cuban Missile Crisis or listening to the laugh track from slapstick comedies. She just sat there staring vacantly into the screen, her thick blond hair swaying almost imperceptibly. Settled in her armchair, she displayed a fierce calmness, like a wild animal driven from her nest. When the late news at eleven was over, his mother would turn off the television and go upstairs to bed. Left alone in the living room, Ben could almost smell her silent torment clinging to the lace curtains like smoky incense.

Houses with parlors were becoming more and more of a rarity, even in the deep South, but all the little clapboard houses on the street where Ben and his mother lived had not only parlors but also long, narrow whitewashed front porches. The house his mother had bought with her divorce settlement was on an old hillside street where many poor white working-class families lived. It was a place where cars from the 1950s sped past rows of houses from the 1920s—a place where weeds, dandelions, and rusty aluminum beer cans were eating away at the asphalt road.

Arlington was an odd "hometown" for Ben to return to. With a population not even half the number of war dead in the national cemetery that bore its name, the town stood at the northernmost point of the South, gazing across the Potomac River to Washington, D.C.

On their side of the bridge, high-rise condominiums that were the residences of high-ranking government officials straddled the highway named after Virginia's own General Robert E. Lee. In the shadows of these high-rises were the vestiges of small Southern hollows. Ben's mother's house was in one of these hollows, halfway down a street that ran through it.

Through the magnolias, Ben could see, one street away, a judge's house that had been built as a replica of Thomas Jefferson's Monticello, replete with Grecian columns. Between the street where his mother's house was and the judge's street was an open space with magnolias, oaks, and willows—trees that found fertile ground in Virginia. It was a long, narrow lot that stretched toward the woods like a plot of land first carved out by white settlers. Railroad ties dating back to the Civil War peeked out like ribs from beneath the fallen yellow and brown leaves.

This open space—the ruins of a railroad—was where the neighborhood boys would gather late at night under the ringleadership of the judge's son. Hidden among the tangle of trees, they learned to smoke, masturbate, and use fancy, cruel words. The empty lot was their nightly stomping ground.

After the late news was over and his mother had gone upstairs to her bedroom, Ben slipped out the back door. This Thursday night near the end of November was not so much cold as it was dead silent. When he got to the bottom of the hillside street, Ben strained his ears. It was quiet enough that he could almost hear the echo of a locomotive long since gone. Loaded with provisions for the Union armies, the ghost train came over the Potomac River and steamed southward, tunneling through the darkness. . . .

The judge's son, who was one year older than Ben, was sitting on a rotted railroad tie. He seemed to be expecting Ben, for he immediately took out a box of unfiltered Chesterfields from his denim jacket and handed a cigarette to Ben and to the boy from the clapboard house next door, who had just gotten there too.

The judge's son lit his own cigarette before lighting the Chesterfields dangling from the mouths of the other boys.

"Three on a match makes a dead nigger," the judge's son whispered, uttering a superstition in that sweet drawl unique to the South.

Acting all manly, the fourteen-year-old judge's son inhaled deeply and blew out a thin, gray line of smoke. To keep from choking, thirteen-year-old Ben and the eleven-year-old neighbor boy didn't inhale, instead letting out big puffs of smoke.

The discarded match smoldered for a moment upon the damp fallen leaves covering the railroad ties. Then the darkness snuffed it out.

After three Chesterfields, Ben went back to his mother's house. He tiptoed from the kitchen into a living room full of shadows. The television was off, as he had left it. But just then, he heard a soft weeping from upstairs. The rhythmic sobs steadily grew louder, eventually washing over the small house like a Gregorian chant filling a Catholic church with melancholy.

SCHOOL LET OUT EARLY ON FRIDAY, AND A COLD RAIN fell all day Saturday as Ben and his mother sat in the living room, their eyes glued to the television. On the Sunday before Thanksgiving, the sky returned to a deep blue, like that of fine English porcelain. Monday was declared a national day of mourning. Shortly after noon that day, Ben left the house alone, lured by the distant sound of a forty-eight-bell carillon.

He followed the old railroad tracks north toward the Potomac River. With the end of November near, the willow branches alongside the tracks drooped lifelessly like light-brown pieces of string. Beneath was trash: a broken bourbon bottle, a car tire, a molding football. Hopping from one railroad tie to the next, Ben soon found himself atop the embankment beside the Robert E. Lee Highway. Across the way, he could see the Sears department store. The front sidewalk was already lined with Christmas trees, but there was no sign of any customers, even though everyone had the day off.

Black people lived in the yellow concrete apartment building along the embankment. Ben had once expressed an interest in going there, but the judge's son warned against it, especially at night. There were no children playing in the front yard, its dead grass gleaming in the autumn sun, and the incongruous sound of televisions blared from almost every window. From a cracked first-floor window with no curtains, a woman about the age of Ben's mother glared at him as he passed by.

After this apartment complex, the carillon of distant bells grew louder. Ben walked on toward the bells.

Crossing an old bridge over the highway, he came upon a crossing signal of what had once been a spur of the railroad. A freight car lay on its side next to the tracks, covered with leaves. He could just make out the large letters SOUTHERN RAILWAY. Stripped of its wheels, it resembled the carcass of a huge bull. Beyond it stretched the waters of the Potomac River, on their way to the Atlantic Ocean. A church steeple in Georgetown towered above the withered trees on the north bank, while the slender outline of Theodore Roosevelt Island floated to the right of Francis Scott Key Bridge. The color of crushed turquoise, the cloudless November sky wrapped around the grayish trees of Washington, D.C., a city inscribed with the names of kings, generals, and presidents. The peal of bells broke through the cool, invigorating air.

Ben quickened his pace, cutting across a parking lot for a high-rise condominium and descending into another hollow. He came to a road, but there were no cars. Passing a country-and-western bar, which had posted a CLOSED sign, and a pawnshop with shotguns displayed in a dusty window, he neared the sound of the bells.

When he reached Route 50, he encountered a river of hundreds of people marching along both sides. People were parking their cars by the side of the road. Everyone was walking toward the bells, silently.

Ben had never seen so many people walking in such complete and utter silence before.

He dashed across the southbound lane, the median, and the northbound lane and then pushed his way toward the front of the crowd, where the bell tower stood atop the yellowish-brown grass. Above the hushed Americans, with their astronaut-inspired crew cuts and bouffant hairdos, a plaintive hymn set to the forty-eight-bell carillon was playing over and over, flowing endlessly like waves on the gray Atlantic Ocean.

On a little mound this side of the bell tower was the memorial to the Battle of Iwo Jima. The larger-than-life bodies and tired, sweat-stained faces of the five Marines trying to raise the Stars and Stripes on the summit of Mount Suribachi in victory were a blaze of green under the afternoon sun.

The Stars and Stripes, which the soldiers were valiantly trying to raise at the end of a ferocious battle, was at half-mast.

THE CROWDS WHO HAD WALKED FROM ROUTE 50 WERE about to join the thousands surrounding the bell tower. Weaving his way between the elbows of the adults, Ben entered Arlington National Cemetery.

That was when the subdued crowd suddenly grew restless. Trampled pages of *The Washington Post* danced about underfoot.

Ben bent down to pick up a page. It had no articles, just black-bordered death notices on both sides. In the middle of the page was a poem, outlined in black. He recognized its antiquated poetic style— maybe he'd been forced to memorize it at the missionary school floating among the rice paddies in that tropical country of his youth, before he knew what America looked like. It read:

O Captain! my Captain! rise up and hear the bells—

It was a poem by Walt Whitman, an elegy written for Abraham Lincoln. As printed, it was like a photograph of the deceased, the framed ornate words from the nineteenth century. For a moment, it looked as if the poem itself had died.

Ben flattened out the crumpled newspaper. In the third stanza of the poem, these words caught his eye:

My father does not feel my arm

Buffeted by the crowds around him—all Americans, all adults—Ben stopped in his tracks on the main approach to the cemetery. The words echoed in his mind, a cloud passed overhead, and for a few brief seconds, the bright sky over Washington, D.C., the Potomac River, and Arlington faded into a fathomless void. From inside the capital came the faint sound of drums.

... my Captain lies,
Fallen cold and dead.
—In memory of John F. Kennedy
November 25, 1963

Ben looked up from the newspaper. Ahead of him, the road went uphill. Beyond that hill was another hill. Like magnolias blooming out of season, hundreds of thousands of white headstones covered the gentle hills as far as the eye could see. Here and there, the sparkle of newly cut marble proclaimed the fact that ordinary people too had died on this late autumn weekend.

Swept along by the sea of people, Ben climbed the slope of headstones that were carved with the names of battlegrounds—from GEORGIA to VIETNAM—where generation after generation of American soldiers had fallen. At last, he reached a point where the road curved, right below the top of the highest hill.

Long limousines drove past the crowds, who were cordoned off behind ropes. Ben caught glimpses of old politicians reclining in the back seats, chatting and puffing on cigars, and then they were gone, like a clip from the *CBS Evening News*.

Standing next to Ben, a man with a crew cut muttered, "Those bastards."

The young president was dead, while the old politicians were alive and well, safe in their shiny black limousines that ascended the hill like hearses.

Through the branches of oak trees arching above the headstones, Ben could see straight down to the Potomac River and the pristine white monuments rising across the capital beyond. Standing on tiptoe at the curve in the uphill road, Ben suddenly felt lightheaded.

The crowds waiting by the side of the road began to stir. The funeral procession had reached the Arlington Memorial Bridge, which spanned the Potomac. The small black limousines and the horses the size of statuettes looked just like a procession of dolls: toy soldiers for the little boy, sad French figurines for the little girl. Slowly, somberly, the tiny procession moved closer.

Once it crossed the bridge, the procession disappeared between the oaks. A few minutes later, it passed before Ben's eyes: the navy honor guard in perfect precision, the jittery riderless horse prancing from side to side, the caisson carrying the coffin draped in a blur of red, white, and blue.

Following the caisson were the world leaders, walking up the hill with waxen faces and leaden feet: Charles de Gaulle next to Emperor Selassie I, Lyndon Johnson and Prince Philip, Ikeda Hayato, Diosdado Macapagal, and Park Chung-hee. . . . Among them were the slain president's brothers Robert Kennedy and Edward Kennedy, and two hundred bodyguards wearing uniforms of every country and every color.

The band began playing "Stars and Stripes Forever."

The scene at the hospital in Texas, which Ben had watched on television at his mother's house—as well as the cheers he had heard coming from the judge's house—came back to him.

"Look!" someone shouted.

Suddenly, there was Jackie Kennedy's face right in front of him. Her veil, hanging down to her waist, was so close it almost brushed Ben's nose. To make sure she was real and not just an image on television, he wanted to reach out, lift up the veil, and touch Jackie's weary, beautiful face.

"Look! Look!"

Jackie, he realized, was leading her three-year-old son, in his shiny red shoes, and her seven-year-old daughter, who had a black ribbon in her hair. Jackie shed not a single tear, her face as pale and frozen as a doll's, making Ben wonder if she was sad or proud to be seen like this by so many people.

Jackie's real face looked surprisingly like the one he had seen on television—in the darkness before dawn, on the screen that ordinarily showed nothing but gray waves. She was wearing the skirt stained with her husband's blood, like dark spots on a pastel kimono, as she stepped down from Air Force One and into the glare of the floodlights. Her face refused to show any emotion, as though she were saying *NO!* to two hundred million Americans.

As Jackie rounded the curve on the approach to the cemetery, the restraint and dignity she conveyed from behind that thin veil were enough to push back the hordes of people pressing against the ropes. The adults around Ben were reduced to silence. Some burst into tears.

Just then, a faint, wry smile seemed to appear on Jackie's frozen lips. *All of you had a hand in this, you know. So save your tears.*

Could she have been thinking this? Ben wondered.

When several people tried to back up at the same time, Ben felt the press of the tightly packed crowd ripple through his small body.

With her two young children in tow, the retreating figure of the widow disappeared around the curve, and a pall of silence fell over the gently sloping hillside in Arlington.

Near the top of the hill, a drumbeat echoed faintly.

Three shots rang out.

It sounded as if the Earth had been shot three times.

YEARS LATER, BEN READ WHAT A POET HAD WRITTEN about that last Monday in November: that it was "the last day Americans shed public tears."

Among the crowds pouring out of the cemetery and heading back to their cars along Route 50, most of the women were crying. This came as little surprise to Ben. But then he witnessed something extraordinary: a man nearly twice Ben's height, with a crew cut, was standing in front of the Iwo Jima memorial and wiping tears from his eyes with large, clumsy hands. For Ben this was a rare glimpse of an astronaut grieving for Earth.

One after the other, Thunderbirds and Chevrolets pulled back onto Route 50 and drove off. The highway at night can be a scary place for a short, solitary pedestrian, so Ben hurried back to the path with the railroad ties and walked toward the hollow. Once he had passed the weathered old crossing signal, which had been left in the STOP position, he made out the line of small clapboard houses. Dusk was beginning to gather, and the far side of the open space was quiet. Even the area around the judge's house—where howls of "That nigger lover got it good" had erupted on Friday afternoon—was completely quiet on this Monday evening. The only sound was the solemn voice of a television newscaster coming through the thin walls of the clapboard houses.

A faint glow lingered in the evening sky. It was that time of day you were supposed to be able to see satellites on the horizon.

He entered the street that led to his mother's house. Through the windows of the houses, he could see families sitting around the television. Some families didn't have fathers, while others didn't have mothers. As he climbed the hill, through the windows of every house Ben could see the same scenes flickering on television screens over and over again:

The White House in the pouring rain, a chandelier wrapped in black crepe.

The calm face of the assassin moments before he was himself assassinated at the basement entrance to the detention room.

The white gloves of the little boy saluting his father's coffin on the stone steps of the cathedral.

The mahogany coffin, bereft of the Stars and Stripes, being lowered into the open grave. . . .

For Ben, as he climbed the hill back to his mother's house, it was like he was flipping through channels. No matter how many times he turned the dial, the program was always the same. Shivering in the cold, he quickened his pace.

When he saw his mother's house, the second from the corner, Ben stopped in his tracks.

A chalky white ambulance had driven up across the narrow sidewalk in front of the house. It stood out vividly, almost blindingly, against the encroaching darkness. The ambulance was parked right in front of the porch.

The door to the house was wide open. Ben could hear the voice of the *CBS Evening News* anchorman. The light from the parlor spilled out onto the whitewashed porch.

Ben knew immediately what had happened.

First, there would have been the sound of a person sobbing. When the "public tears" had ended, a single, quieter sobbing would have continued alone, trapped in the upstairs bedroom.

Ben was well acquainted with that sound.

After the late news, when his mother had turned off the television and gone upstairs to bed, he would often hear that sound. Trickling down the stairs until it filled the entire house, that forlorn pain—like a dam about to burst—was all too familiar to his ears.

Late at night, he would lie awake in his bedroom on the first floor, listening to the cadence of the sobs.

When he heard his father's name slip out between the sobs, it was like a gun going off behind him: Ben would jump up in bed and listen for the sound again.

In the chilly darkness on this last Monday in November, Ben hid behind the trunk of a large oak tree on the sidewalk, peering out at the ambulance and the light in the second-story window. The shadows of two men passed across the window like spasmodic television waves.

Probably, one of the neighbors had phoned the hospital. Turning into the street from the Lee Highway, the ambulance would drive up to the house without its siren—for they had done this before—and cut across the sidewalk. Two men in white coats would get out of the ambulance and take slow, methodical steps across the porch and into the parlor. After flinching upon seeing the Buddha and the Kutani-ware platter on the bookcase above the television, they would climb the stairs, leaving a trail of antiseptic smell like sour cologne. It was always the same two guys. When they got to the top of the stairs, the one behind—a stocky fellow—would get out a long syringe, while the one in front—a thin doctor wearing glasses—would call out in a coaxing, Southern accent.

"Mrs. Isaac, please."

The sobbing would cease. Then there would come a fierce "No!"

After a pause, in an assured tone, his mother's voice would be heard to say: "I am perfectly normal." And then the neurotic ravings would begin.

The doctor would quietly approach and try to grab her arm.

"I told you, I am perfectly normal. Go get Jacob!" she would scream, blurting out the name of Ben's father.

When the stocky fellow entered the bedroom, the doctor would instruct him: "Hold on to her shoulders."

Another shriek: "No!"

71

As she sat on the bed, the slightly flabby skin around her neck would be quivering. Her waitress uniform would be hanging next to the bed.

"I'm the victim here. Go get Jacob, not me!"

The two men in white would greet his mother's protests with smiles, as if to say: *Yes, you're the victim and the loser, which is precisely why you're not normal. In this state, you're the one who should be put away.* Without breaking his smile or his gentle tone of voice, the doctor would roll up his mother's sleeve, preparing to administer a sedative.

The moment the alcohol swab touched her arm, Ben's mother would stop resisting.

The shadows of the men flickering in the second-floor window disappeared. A momentary scream shot through the clapboard wall and ricocheted off the sidewalk.

From the darkness of the South, the sound of a locomotive whistle rang in Ben's ears as he hid behind the oak tree.

He heard footsteps hurrying down the stairs. Supported by the two men in white coats, his mother came out onto the porch. The porch light turned her thick blond hair into a golden veil. She looked like a beautiful widow leaning on two men who were helping her into a hearse.

Ben wanted to run to his mother's side and touch her dazed, weary face, but he hesitated, as if the massive tree trunk were holding him back.

Gleaming in the night, the chalky white ambulance slowly drove off toward the Lee Highway, crossing the railroad tracks where a train would never come, no matter how long you waited.

A SUDDEN, LOUD CRESCENDO—DVOŘÁK'S "NEW WORLD Symphony," perhaps—roused Ben from his reverie.

The rain had ended, and the light from the street filtered through the whisky-colored window, condensing into a single bright line that penetrated the interior space. Illuminating the dust and the cigarette smoke, the light fell like epaulettes on the customers' shoulders.

Fugetsudo was packed. The round tables along the first-floor passageway were filled with the bobbing heads of black-haired customers trying to talk over the tumult of the Dvořák. Two women in jeans were nodding to each other about something serious (*"Sō na no?"* *"Sō na no yo!"*), next to a prematurely balding European man expounding on Buddhist enlightenment (*"Satori, satori"*) to a circle of Japanese students.

Ben crumpled his empty cigarette box into a ball and left it on the table as he stood up from his chair. He glanced over at the refugee girl and then went downstairs. Skirting the beam of light, he passed through the gazes of several dozen people. With two hundred-yen bills and a handful of coins, he paid for his coffee and then left the café. He'd been there for seven hours.

Even outside, Ben moved through people's gazes. Their eyes focused immediately on him, as though they had been lying in wait for him. Through the alternating looks of curiosity, resentment, admiration, and contempt he saw in their eyes, Ben walked on.

At the corner of the willow-lined avenue, he ducked into a side street. He was hungry, but he didn't feel like going into any of the places he passed: the eateries, the cafés, the pubs with their red lanterns already glowing despite the daylight still left in the sky. That day, Ben didn't feel like answering the questions that someone would always throw at him whenever he entered such places:

"Where are you from, kiddo?"

"What are you doing here, kiddo?"

"Why don't you go back where you belong, kiddo?"

On this day near the end of November, Ben didn't have the energy.

At a main thoroughfare, he turned left. Without anywhere to go, Ben kept walking, letting his feet take him where they would. He found himself at the east entrance of the station. A ragtag group of vagrants was camped there like an army of brightly colored snails. On top of a truck, a man in a uniform stood waving his fist and hurling a soliloquy at the sky, now a deeper shade of blue.

Turning around, Ben spotted a narrow alley, which he entered, fighting his way through the crowd of people coming toward him. He reached another avenue, where he darted among the Toden streetcars passing beneath a maze of aerial wires bouncing in the autumn wind. Safely on the other side, he continued downhill along an awning-covered sidewalk.

He came out onto a plaza. Theaters and movie houses surrounded it on all four sides. From the wall of a theater, the huge face of a female singer in a kimono gazed down on him triumphantly.

Alleys and side streets flowed into the plaza from all directions.

Eventually, even the hillside street in that hollow back in Arlington would flow into this plaza. And here it would end. Or so Ben thought as he stopped before the theater.

Making his way to the fountain in the middle of the plaza, he felt as though he had been walking for years before finally reaching this place. Like him, many other runaways had found themselves here. Alongside the pimps and the prostitutes, they stared at him blatantly, looking more curious than suspicious. Under their watchful eyes, Ben lay down on a bench beside the fountain.

He stuck his hand in his pocket to see how much money he had left. 2,500 yen. And no ID card.

Shokudō ga suite kitara, doko ka ni hairō, Ben said to himself in Japanese. *I'll find a place to eat when it gets less crowded.*

He turned his eyes from the mosaic of neon signs and flashy billboards dancing in the fountain and looked up at the sky of SHIN-JU-KU, which had turned an even deeper blue, almost black. The cold from the bench seeped into his body.

A number of bells rang out in unison, announcing that the movies were about to start.

As he turned toward the deafening sound, Ben sensed the word "November" beginning to fall apart inside his head.

ONE OF THE GUYS

I

HE SAT UP UNDER THE QUILT AND FUMBLED AROUND FOR the key on the windowsill. Feeling like he was tampering with the lock on a treasure chest, he turned the key three times and the window popped open, affording Ben a view of an undulating ocean of blue and gray roof tiles. Among the endless waves of second-story roofs, taller buildings stood out, catching the pink glow from the setting sun. As Ben's eyes traveled up the hillside, the buildings got closer and closer together. Where the roof tiles and the concrete ended, two small lights—then a third—lit up in a row, like the stars in Orion's belt. They were the lights Andō had pointed to on that autumn evening, when he gave a skittish laugh and told Ben, "One of these days, I'll take ya to Shinjuku."

The time of day had arrived for Ben to head out to his job in SHIN-JU-KU.

Basking in the daylight, he looked around the room. Without Andō, who had been gone all afternoon, the four-and-a-half–mat room felt spacious, even though it was littered with books, records, and an empty NIKKA whisky bottle. Driven by a need to fill the space that had previously been occupied by Andō's large body, Ben's gaze wandered over Andō's stuff scattered about, finally stopping at the wall opposite the window.

Andō's school uniform was hanging on the wall. Bulky and black as night, the uniform reigned over the four-and-a-half–mat room, where the last light of day was waning. Wrapped in a quilt from his waist down, Ben slowly pulled himself over toward the wall.

Inside the room and out in the hallway, it was deathly quiet.

He looked up at the uniform, thinking back to that autumn evening when he had walked through the alleys of Tokyo for the first time, chasing after the back of Andō's black uniform.

Ben was seized by a sudden impulse.

I want to wear Andō's uniform.

I want to put that baggy black suit of armor on my scrawny white body and leave Andō's boardinghouse with it on. Then I want to join the hordes of uniforms, swarming the streets around W University. I want to melt into the mass of them and disappear. . . .

Ben reached up and touched the uniform. The material was surprisingly coarse. Grazing the chest pocket, he undid the top button. His fingers traced over the difficult *kanji* stamped onto the button. The other three buttons glimmered in the shadows.

From the landlord's house next door, Ben could hear a piano and a high-pitched voice, like a child making fun of someone.

Don't do it, a voice in Japanese told him from somewhere in his head. Leaving the top button undone, Ben drew his hand away from Andō's uniform.

He stood up, kicking off the quilt, and quickly put on his own clothes: blue jeans, a flannel shirt, and a blue jacket over that. With his head still half-asleep, he shuffled into the hallway.

He went down to the first floor and stood before the washbasin, picking up the razor that Andō always left under the mirror. It was a small razor, the kind they sold at public baths for twenty yen, in a package secured with a rubber band. As Andō would do, Ben splashed cold water on his face and rubbed the soap to create some foam. Although the razor blade had become dull from so much use on Andō's broad face, the moment it touched Ben's cheek, he was fully awake.

The image in the mirror gradually assumed the contours of a Caucasian face. Startled, Ben blurted out, "Ah, a *gaijin*." He was looking at an exceedingly pale white face. It was a face completely different from Andō's and those he saw in SHIN-JU-KU. This was not the first time that he had been shocked to see his own face since leaving the consulate.

After Ben ran away from home, Andō told him, "Since ya got nobody else to stay with, I'll let ya stay here with me for a while." He must have felt sorry for the pale white face at his door.

That face also resembled his father's. Every time Ben saw his own blue-gray eyes, which shone with intensity underneath a massive forehead, Ben felt like his father was watching him. Then he would hear his father's words echoing through his mind: "Even if you go to the plaza in front of the Imperial Palace and scream 'Long live the Emperor!' in perfect Japanese and slit your stomach open, you'll never be one of *them*."

Since running away from home, Ben made every effort not to look at mirrors.

The smell of fish grilling next door wafted through the boardinghouse, assaulting Ben's senses.

He wiped his face with Andō's towel and went into the entryway. From among the jumble of black shoes near the front door, he immediately spotted his big brown loafers, which his mother had bought for him in Virginia the previous year. They were fairly worn down now. If nothing else, Ben's feet were bigger than Andō's.

Out on the avenue, he passed under a sign that read YAMAZAKI BREAD in *katakana* and bought one cream-filled roll and two bean-jam doughnuts. The first "My, what lovely Japanese you speak" of the day was handed to him along with his change. With the words *O-jōzu desu ne* still ringing in his ears, he tore into the cream-filled roll.

Every day, after getting up when the evening sun was hitting the window of Andō's room, he would hand thirty-five yen to the girl behind the cash register under the YAMAZAKI BREAD sign and buy his "breakfast." And every day, the same girl would tell him, *O-jōzu desu ne.* Trying to avoid the inevitable follow-up questions that would come if he stayed any longer, Ben would nod, give an ambiguous "Japanese smile," and hurry away to the safety of the sidewalk.

Biting into a bean-jam doughnut, he turned left at the police box at the intersection. Above the concrete block of the Department of Literature, the evening sky had clouded over. In groups of three and four, W University students spilled out the gate. Swarms of black hair, black school uniforms, and black shoes swept past Ben. Ignoring the two or three *harro*s that fell at his feet, he proceeded past the gate and into the deeper shadows of the trees. The darkness offering him camouflage, Ben felt relief and a kind of joy.

Where the trees ended, beyond the apartment complex on the hill, were the lights of SHIN-JU-KU, suspended like gold dust on the horizon.

He entered the large park at the foot of the hill and began climbing up the path Andō had shown him. The light from streetlights illuminated the path faintly. Along the way, flecks of fine snow began drifting through the light.

Just beyond the apartment complex, a torrent of cold, blinding light struck Ben's eyes. He had made it to the main drag.

Unlike the streets he had walked until this point, Ben knew the name of this big street. He hadn't learned it from Andō. He had picked it up himself in the process of going back and forth between Andō's room and SHIN-JU-KU.

Meiji-dōri. Meiji Avenue. It sucked the light into SHIN-JU-KU and carried it away too. Every night, when he was exposed to that light, having taken the path through the park, Ben would feel a shudder of euphoria and instinctively quicken his step. Unnoticed, he fell in among the crowds of people rushing along the sidewalk of Meiji Avenue toward SHIN-JU-KU, which now seemed close enough to touch.

Within five or six minutes, Meiji Avenue gradually sloped downhill. At the bottom, he could see the road split. The long pedestrian bridge spanning the divide was dazzlingly white in the fine snow. Just before that point, a Toden streetcar jerked to the right and disappeared around a curve. Ben followed it, treading along the tracks that snaked between two-story buildings on either side. It was not yet night, but the sounds of jazz and mournful Japanese ballads were already in the air. On a rack outside a second-floor apartment, laundry hung under the fresh coating of snow; someone had neglected to take it in. In the opposite window, Ben watched a woman watch him as he carefully made his way along the whitened tracks toward her.

The woman was about fifty and had the air of a bar madam. From the window, she showed only her heavily made-up face and the shoulder of her satin dress. Perhaps she was killing time, admiring the snow, until her bar opened.

Without thinking, Ben prepared himself for another *harro*.

The snow fell like a veil before the woman's face. When Ben was directly under her window, the woman's red lips hesitated behind the veil, as though unsure what language to address him in. Then, in Japanese, she called out to him, "Cold, ain't it?"

It was a man's voice!

Ben's jaw dropped. For a moment, he couldn't think straight, the words in his head getting all mixed up. Looking up at the drag queen staring down at him as though waiting for an answer, Ben let loose the only words he could think of for such a situation.

"You can say that again."

Hearing the voice of a Japanese person come out of Ben's mouth, the drag queen laughed raspily. "You sure can, sister," he said.

It was the laugh of a kindred spirit. It sounded as if the man, who lived as a woman, had seen through to Ben's real identity. At the same time, it sounded like a note of approval for the role that Ben was performing.

Feeling the man's gaze on his back—the man who had shed his male identity—Ben quickened his pace. Crossing the tracks, he turned right, slipping in among the crowds of Japanese at the entrance to the Golden Gai district, and hurried off to work.

2

FOR TWO OR THREE DAYS BEFORE HE RAN AWAY FROM the consulate, Ben had holed himself up in his room, not speaking to either his father or his father's wife, reading a novel about a boy who stuttered.

It was a novel written by the author who wore a military uniform in the photograph Andō had stuck on his wall. The English translation had an illustration of a golden Chinese phoenix engulfed in flames on the cover.

Ben had never read a Japanese novel before. In his father's study, which was next to Ben's bedroom, there were rows and rows of dusty old books on topics like Chinese philosophy and Oriental history. But he couldn't find a single Japanese novel among them, with the exception of *Kwaidan* and *Kottō* by Koizumi Yakumo.

The Stars and Stripes filled the window, waving in the wind coming off the harbor and across Yamashita Park. With the flag flapping in the background, Ben turned the pages of the *The Temple of the Golden Pavilion*. It was the paperback edition, the title embossed in gold above the image of the phoenix on fire. He read carefully, his eyes lingering on each and every short paragraph, like the way he had savored every puff from the first cigarette he smoked in middle school.

The stutterer's name was Mizoguchi. Ben found himself reading the parts describing Mizoguchi over and over again:

The first sound is like a key....

Mizoguchi would stutter on the first syllable. *That first sound is like a key to the door between my inner world and the outer world, but the key always seems to get stuck in the lock.*

When he stumbled on that first syllable and began stuttering, he was: *like a little bird struggling....*

As the author in the military uniform wrote, he was *like a little bird struggling to free itself from thick birdlime. By the time it finally breaks free, it is too late.*

It is too late. Ben tried to envision the face of the stutterer at that moment of realization, but he came up empty-handed.

AS HE READ, BEN HEARD FAINT FOOTSTEPS. THEY WERE slow and steady, the steps of many people. He looked out the window. Down on Yamashita Park Avenue, several Japanese were approaching the iron fence around the consulate.

Ben put the book down and closed his eyes. In place of the stutterer's hazy, indistinct face, the photograph of the author he'd seen in Andō's room floated up in his mind. The photograph was stuck on the wall next to Andō's school uniform. Ben could vividly recall the small face and the stern gaze it cast over the room from under the visor of a military cap.

The gaze was more than just stern. It gave the odd impression that the man's eyes were stuttering slightly, unable to articulate another kind of emotion, distinct from sternness. Now, as Ben sat in the consulate and remembered the face in that photograph, this impression only got stronger.

Through the flapping of the Stars and Stripes, the sounds of Japanese people conversing as they walked by the consulate floated up to his bedroom on the second floor, their rhythmic laughs coming and going in waves.

For people who stutter, Ben thought, the voices of people who don't stutter must sound like the language he heard spoken by the Japanese outside the consulate.

Even after running away from the consulate and arriving in SHIN-JU-KU, Ben often thought of Mizoguchi the stutterer. *The first sound is like a key. . . .*

When Ben spoke to strangers in SHIN-JU-KU, the problems would arise from the very first word that left his mouth. The moment the other person realized that Ben was speaking Japanese, not English, a look of surprise would invariably come across the person's face. The rest of Ben's Japanese seemed to fall on deaf ears, perhaps from the shock of that first word. As soon as Ben opened his mouth, it was like the key that was beginning to turn would suddenly get stuck in the lock. The other person would scowl at him in silence or fling phrases at him like "My, what lovely Japanese you speak" or "Wow, your Japanese is pretty good," without acknowledging what Ben was trying to say and switching the topic of conversation to the simple fact that a pale-faced foreigner was speaking Japanese.

Ever since Andō told him, "You're in Japan, man, so speak Japanese," Ben had been trying to speak the language. As he walked the alleys and sloping streets around W University, tagging along behind Andō, he soon forgot that the stream of sounds coming from his own mouth was Japanese. Maybe those sounds became Japanese for the first time only when he forgot what language he was speaking in. Andō's injunction to *speak Japanese* carried an undertone of *forget.* It was as though Andō were ordering him to *forget English, forget America, forget all of it—whatever it was that happened to you in America.* Indeed, as long as Ben listened to Andō's Japanese and replied in his own clumsy Japanese, he was able to forget those things.

Once he got to SHIN-JU-KU, however, Ben discovered that, unlike Andō, the Japanese people he met would not let him forget. No, they were worried about what might happen if he did forget. What Ben encountered was not just stony silence and false praise. When these people detected the slightest hint of a desire to forget in the first word from Ben's mouth, they became anything but silent. At times, they subjected him to a barrage of broken English—far worse than Ben's Japanese—with the fervor of someone throwing rocks at an intruder.

Like the speech of a stutterer in reverse, the smoother the words flowing from Ben's mouth became, the more they backed up behind people's shock and disbelief, flooding Ben's inner world. By the time Ben quickly rephrased himself in Japanese, it was too late.

Because he was not allowed to forget, his words were always a little too late.

BEN RAN AWAY FROM HOME ON A DAY NEAR THE END OF November. After wandering around SHIN-JU-KU all day, he made it to a plaza just as night was falling. In the middle of the plaza was a fountain. When he lay down on a bench near the fountain, the sea of lights in the plaza came on, and a cold wind skimmed over the surface of the fountain, ruffling the water like thousands of pebbles thrown in at the same time and wetting the cuff of his pants with neon-colored spray.

The opening bells of the movie houses, which surrounded the fountain on three sides, rang out in unison. After the bells ended, a few seconds of silence ensued in the bustling plaza. Just as he felt his consciousness growing dimmer, the voices of the people around him grew strangely louder, each of them becoming more pronounced.

Stranger still, at that moment he got the feeling that he could understand the many Japanese voices around him. It was as though his own voice were echoing off the walls of the buildings around him, multiplying into different Japanese voices—words ending with *da*, *yo*, *wa*, and *ze*—that saturated the sky above the darkening plaza.

The chill from the bench seeped into his body. Ben began to shiver. Interspersed with the gurgling of the fountain, Japanese voices filled his ears, making him wonder where "November" had gone even as they urged him to *forget*.

With a faint smile, Ben closed his eyes and drifted in and out of consciousness.

He awoke in the plaza before dawn, finding himself looking up at rays of white light in the irregular rectangle of sky overhead.

The sound of the first train of the day reverberated through the plaza.

When he got up from the bench, he felt light, as though a heavy, nameless burden had lifted from his shoulders during the night.

Ah, the crisp, clean air of SHIN-JU-KU! Ben slowly looked around the plaza. The fountain had stopped. On the benches around it, on the stone steps leading up to it, people were sleeping, cocooned in ragged quilts and old newspapers. Over in front of the theater, a few men dressed in workmen's clothes were squatting in a circle, their hands busily playing some kind of card game. From within the circle, a cry of A-KA-TAN rose up, breaking the silence of the plaza. Someone had scored a "triple red."

As soon as he stood up, Ben went weak at the knees. He felt like he was leaving his own corpse behind. The seventeen-year-old son of the American consul who wandered into a SHIN-JU-KU plaza one late November evening, his life cut short beside a fountain. The young Yankee who never did go home, his face as pale as bones.

I gotta get outta here before someone sees me, Ben thought. He quickly rushed down the steps of the fountain, zipping his jacket all the way up, and then cut across the plaza toward the theater.

Under the billboard of the kimono-clad singer adorning the theater wall, Ben passed by several people in black and brown overcoats. For some reason, they didn't strike him as Japanese, or *Nihonjin*, as they had the previous day. Moreover, he detected only slight looks of surprise on their faces as he walked among them.

Perhaps it was the nature of the place called SHIN-JU-KU, but everyone looked like they were here because they too had run away from home. Was the SHIN-JU-KU Andō spoke of a place for people who had no home to go to? A Japanese voice—reminiscent of Andō's but unmistakably his own—welled up in Ben's head. *Ore wa koko ni iru beki da*, it proclaimed. *I belong here.*

Ben ventured into a side street that came down to the plaza from the Toden streetcar tracks in a long, gentle slope. He walked past an arcade. A little farther, at the corner of another alley, a white neon sign came into view. In the pale light of morning, he couldn't be sure if the neon sign was on or off. It was for a café. In Gothic letters, the sign read: CASSLE.

Under the sign was a poster taped to the glass door. The dark red *kanji* jumped out at him:

月一万五千円

¥15,000 a month!

After stalling, making two trips up and down the side street and a circle through the alleys, Ben returned to Cassle. The day had gotten brighter. He stood there for a while, afraid to go in. Emboldened by the dark red promise of "¥15,000 a month," he finally opened the door.

The first thing he noticed was the huge chandelier. There was a mezzanine at the top of a wide staircase, and it too had a chandelier. For a moment, Ben was back in the entrance hall of the consulate. But the chandeliers here were made of milky white plastic, unlike the translucent crystal of the consulate. Both plastic chandeliers were off. The only source of light was the few rays of natural sunlight spilling in from the glass door.

Alone at the cash register was a middle-aged man flipping through a stack of receipts. There were speakers mounted on the wall behind him, but no music was playing. Maybe the customers and employees had all left? There was not a sign of anyone besides the middle-aged man, who looked younger than Ben's father.

Following a ray of light, Ben walked up to the register. He lowered his head, preparing to speak.

Standing there blocking the feeble light from outside, Ben had barely opened his mouth when the middle-aged man grabbed the stack of receipts—seemingly worried that he had been caught red-handed—and frantically shooed Ben away with the word *ku-roh-zu*. Closed.

Ben took a step back, Japanese words rising in his throat. "Um," he said, uttering the first sound.

A look of surprise began to surface on the man's face. Before it started spreading across the man's long, narrow, nicotine-stained face, from his forehead to his five-o'clock shadow, Ben spat out the rest of the sentence in one breath.

"Excuse me, but I saw the BO-SHŪ sign outside."

In the ensuing silence, Ben could hear his voice hit the plastic chandeliers and scatter across the room in a shower of echoes.

The middle-aged man, however, might not have heard anything past the first syllable, for his face remained frozen in shock. Gradually, the shock gave way to confusion. In a shaky voice, neither scolding nor beseeching, he kept saying, *Ku-roh-zu, ku-roh-zu*, waving his hand wildly, as if to drive away the figure in front of him.

"I want to work here."

Ben tried to say it another way, but his voice had lost its strength. *It is too late.* Ben realized this in English even as he said those words in Japanese. What language did the man think he was speaking? Crestfallen, Ben mumbled, "Sorry to have bothered you," and awkwardly stepped back toward the glass door.

Once Ben moved away from the register, the man stopped waving his hand and breathed a sigh of relief.

When Ben had retreated to the door, the man suddenly bowed. Even though he was more than twice Ben's age, he bowed deeply and gushed, "*Ohh, san-kyū.*" A Japanese-style "thank you."

Turning his back on the man at last, Ben pushed the glass door open. From behind him, he heard the man's voice getting louder and louder, like someone reciting an incantation:

Ohh, san-kyū, Kenne-dee, erai, guddo-bai. Thank you, Kennedy is great, good-bye.

When he left Cassle and stepped back onto the side street, morning light was pouring in from the plaza and there was the sound of shutters rattling open. Outside the arcade, two young male employees, about the same age as Ben, were diligently getting the place ready to open.

When they happened to see the figure of Ben standing alone on the paving stones, which were clearly outlined in the light, they stopped and stared. This really bothered Ben anew, so reluctantly he got going and dragged his feet toward the Toden streetcar tracks.

He dug around in his pants pocket. All that was there were three bills of different sizes—and, he reminded himself, no "ticket to extraterritoriality." Rolling around at the bottom were a few coins, cold to the touch. Some of them were thin, with holes in the middle.

As he stepped carefully from paving stone to paving stone, testing the ground beneath his feet, Ben thought, *What if I went back to the consulate now?* The consulate was his father's house. It belonged to his father, his father's wife, and their black-haired baby boy, his half-brother. Before he ran away from *their* home, Ben would sometimes spend so much time in Andō's room that he wouldn't show up at the consulate until *they* were almost done with dinner. When that happened, his father would threaten to send him back to Virginia, back to his mother's house. As his father had reminded him, again and again, Ben was a "dependent." As in the opposite of "independent." His father had the right to kick him out of Japan at any time. Whenever he told that to Ben, his father—who was born and bred in Brooklyn—would use a peculiar Southern expression and threaten to *pluck you off like a bad leaf, son.*

This time, though, Ben hadn't been to his father's house for almost three days.

He wondered if his father was looking for him yet. Had he summoned his Japanese secretary to his office and had her interpret his demand for an immediate investigation by the Japanese authorities?

Kenne-dee, erai. Ben spat loudly onto the paving stones. Yeah, Kennedy's great. Up ahead, at the top of the side street, he could see a flashy arch that signaled the entrance to Kabuki-chō in *kanji*. Beyond the sea of black-haired heads flowing past the arch on their way from the train station to the city streets, Toden streetcars and buses kept going by. The Toden streetcar tracks were just a few feet away.

At the arch, the crowd split apart, and a bunch of people came walking toward Ben, who was alone.

It is too late.

Ben felt the gazes of several dozen people wash over him all at once.

He froze. He could feel what each of them was thinking: *What are you doing here?*

Ben looked over his shoulder in shame, wishing he could disappear. Then he broke into a run and fled down a long alley cutting across Kabuki-chō.

THAT NIGHT, BEN RETURNED TO CASSLE, THIS TIME WITH Andō by his side.

He showed Andō the dark red kanji that read "¥15,000 a month."

"Hey, not bad," Andō said, and opened the glass door without a moment's hesitation.

When Ben made to follow him in, Andō turned around and stopped him. "You wait out here."

Ben stood by himself on the side street. Here and there, neon signs sputtered to life. Peering through the glass door, Ben could barely see what was happening under the light of the plastic chandeliers. Like Ben had done that morning, Andō was lowering his buzz-cut head and talking to the middle-aged man at the register. Sometimes together and sometimes separately, they nodded, laughed, looked serious, and then began to argue. Two or three times during their conversation, Andō pointed to Ben standing outside the glass door, but the more Andō pleaded his case, the more the middle-aged man resisted. As he watched the debate become more heated, Ben started to feel left out in the cold, like he was watching a war of words that had nothing to do with him on the other side of the murky glass.

A pair of hands flashed through the milky light. Andō seemed to be pointing at the badge on the collar of his school uniform. Then he took out a card from his chest pocket—his student ID card, perhaps—and showed it to the middle-aged man, apparently trying to persuade him of something.

A few minutes later, the middle-aged man and Andō both calmed down and began to confer quietly. When it was all over, Andō once again lowered his buzz-cut head to the middle-aged man. Unlike in the morning, the middle-aged man just nodded, making no effort to bow back.

When Andō came out through the glass door, he flashed Ben a "V" sign. But his eyes were downcast and he was holding back a smile, like he had heard a stupid joke. Ben had not expected this.

"What's wrong?" Ben asked.

Andō remained silent, reluctant to respond.

Ben tried to read the expression on Andō's face, but Andō avoided his eyes. He looked around for a full three seconds before blurting out:

"I ended up becomin' your *hoshōnin.*"

"HO-SHŌ-NIN?"

Andō frowned, his mind running through the entrance-exam English vocabulary he had begun to forget. "Someone who guarantees," he added.

"Guarantees? Guarantees what?"

"Guarantees you," Andō replied, with a sheepish grin on his face.

"*Nan de?*" Why?

Andō looked down, seeming to have more he didn't want to say, and stared intently at the paving stones. Following Andō's gaze, Ben discovered fantastic shadows playing across the paving stones. Finally, Andō finally mumbled, "He said ya gotta have someone who'll vouch for ya."

The Japanese phrase *nan de* rose to the back of Ben's throat again, but he forced it back down.

Andō grabbed Ben's elbow and pulled him away from Cassle. When they got to the long alley cutting through Kabuki-chō into which Ben had fled that morning, Andō turned around and glanced at Ben. Andō didn't say anything, but Ben knew that Andō saw him as an oddity—as someone who couldn't survive in Japan without a HO-SHŌ-NIN. In Andō's eyes, Ben caught a glimpse of pity for the first time.

The alley went on, crossing one large side street and numerous small ones. Pimps lined the alley, beckoning to everyone who passed by. When they saw Andō, they called out, "Mr. Student" or "Only 3,000 yen," but when they saw Ben walking behind Andō, they laughed and shouted, "*Hay yoo*" or "*Japaneezu pusshee*." Through the breezy banter, Ben and Andō walked in silence.

When they got to the end of the alley, beneath the towering yellow walls of the ward office, Andō turned to Ben. "Oh yeah," he mumbled, as if suddenly remembering, "be there by seven tomorrow night."

YOROSHIKU ONEGAI ITASHIMASU.

Standing in front of the middle-aged man he had been told to call Manager, Ben nervously pronounced each syllable of the formal greeting Andō had taught him.

The Manager said nothing in response and displayed something between a condescending grin and a disagreeable grimace on his long, narrow "horse face," as Andō described it. He motioned for Ben to follow him and silently began climbing the dark stairs at the back of the mezzanine, where the light from the chandeliers didn't reach.

To the left of the second-floor landing was a dimly lit entrance with a burgundy velvet curtain screening off the interior. Never breaking his businesslike stride, the Manager charged up the stairs to the third floor.

"What was that room over there?" Ben asked.

An unfamiliar Japanese word came tumbling down the narrowing, ladderlike stairs, which were half-lit by a naked yellow light bulb on the third floor.

"DŌ-HAN-SHI-TSU."

The Manager sounded annoyed.

On the third floor was a dressing room lined with dark green lockers. Without a word, the Manager opened the locker on the far left. There was a well-starched set of clothes on a hanger.

"Is this my uniform?" Ben asked.

Perhaps his mousy, high-pitched voice in Japanese had simply rubbed the Manager the wrong way, as several wrinkles appeared across the man's forehead, which looked noticeably larger in the yellow glare. Speaking not so much to Ben as to a point in space, he barked, "*Putto on, putto on.*" The Manager made a buttoning-up gesture and pointed to the stairs. The message was: "When you're done changing, come downstairs." Then the Manager hurried down the stairs like someone who has just completed an unpleasant chore.

Alone in the dressing room, Ben stared at the white uniform hanging in the locker. He stood in a daze, unmoving. Looking up, he saw pink, blue, and purple lights fluttering in the tiny air vent. One after another, the neon lights along the side street were reflecting off the windowpane like *pachinko* balls randomly hitting each other, lending an impression of warmth to the otherwise cold, unheated dressing room. The swelling strains of a Japanese ballad sung by a woman flowed up from the DŌ-HAN-SHI-TSU, the "date room." The only words in the lyrics that he could understand were *watashi dake*, "I alone," which were repeated over and over.

Ben took off his loafers and slowly unbuttoned the flannel shirt his mother had bought for him in Virginia a year earlier. He felt a thrill of excitement mixed with fear. Even before taking off his shirt and jeans, he felt naked. He had never felt this naked before.

He removed the jacket of the uniform from the locker and held it up to the light. The white material was badly faded, having a faint pinkish glow to it, like the skin on his own bony arms exposed to the cold. The area around the collar was frayed. How many other people—how many other runaways with bony arms like his—had worn this uniform before him? How many other people had come here, casting aside the clothes their parents had bought for them to work the night shift in SHIN-JU-KU, where the daily rhythms they once shared with their parents were turned upside down?

Ben took off his flannel shirt and slipped the jacket on. The size was just right. He buttoned it up to the collar and looked down at the white armor covering his chest. Small red letters, in English, were sewn above the chest pocket: CASSLE. It took him a few seconds, but Ben finally realized that the spelling was wrong; it should have been CASTLE. But he liked it that way. In Japanese, Ben whispered it to himself: *Kyassuru*. It sounded smooth, pleasurable, sophisticated.

He changed into the pants and threw his American clothes in the locker.

He looked down the long staircase leading to the mezzanine. It was less intimidating than before.

3

THE GUY HAD A SALLOW COMPLEXION, BUT IT WAS probably not just because he always stood in the circle of white light emanating from the plastic chandeliers. The guy looked unhealthy, but he didn't look weak. On the contrary, there was even something tough about him. He was not yet twenty years old, but he seemed like an old pro at the late-night waiter routine, judging from the way he could stand for hours in the same position without leaving his station on the mezzanine.

When Ben descended the stairs and appeared on the mezzanine for the first time, the guy was waiting for him.

At first, the guy, who was wearing a similar white uniform, managed to fake a smile at Ben. But when Ben turned toward him, the fake smile disappeared. As Ben approached the waiter station—its counter neatly arranged with water glasses and freshly washed ashtrays—the guy flinched and took a step back.

Faced by someone who flinched at his very approach, Ben was at a loss for words. Hurriedly, he tried to introduce himself, but he had never introduced himself in Japanese to anyone before. No matter how much he racked his brains, the only phrase that came to mind was the one from the chapter on "Meeting Someone for the First Time" in the Japanese-language textbook he'd been forced to study at W University. Knowing that it was probably not the best way to address the guy, who was recoiling in terror, he declared:

"Nice to meet you. My name is Ben Isaac."

The second he said this, Ben felt ashamed. For some reason, he was embarrassed to utter such a formal, deferential greeting, which he had never used with Andō.

The guy didn't seem to pick up on Ben's embarrassment. At the very sight of Ben, he had shrunk back, as if to hide behind the counter. There was no way the guy could know what it felt like to be treated that way and lose one's balance, not knowing what to say. After Ben said, "Nice to meet you," the guy said nothing, his eyes alternating between Ben's white uniform—no different from his—and Ben's face—so different from his.

The guy stared at Ben with no expression on his anemic face. Almost disciplined in its perfection, the guy's silence resounded in Ben's ears.

After a minute had passed, Ben couldn't take it anymore. Since he was the newbie, the underling, the junior, or—as Andō would say—the *kōhai*, Ben thought he should be the one answering the questions, not asking them. Having no choice, he ventured, "And your name is . . . ?" Realizing immediately that he'd forgotten to use the honorific prefix *o* with the word for "name" when talking to a superior, Ben frantically tried to say it again, but the guy had already begrudgingly moved his lips and mumbled:

"MA-SU-MU-RA."

The moment he announced his name, a tiny spasm shot across the surface of the guy's otherwise expressionless face. Could it be that the guy was afraid of Ben for some reason, that he wasn't as tough as he looked? No, that would be absurd, that would be *ridiculous*, Ben thought in English.

The guy fell silent again.

If he didn't work next to this guy every night from eight o'clock to six the next morning, that dark red "¥15,000 a month" would never materialize. This was too depressing. He had to do something to ease this tension—but what? Suddenly he hit upon the guy's name. It began like other names he'd seen in his Japanese-language textbook or the piles of publications in Andō's room: MA-SU-DA, MA-SU-YA-MA, MA-SU-. . . He even vaguely remembered the shape of the *kanji*, which meant "to increase."

Remembering how Andō had once taught him a certain Japanese character—ages ago, it now seemed—by tracing it on the palm of his hand, Ben stuck his hand out to the guy. This time, it was Ben who drew the character onto his palm, a rough approximation of *masu*—増—followed by the character for *mura*—村—which meant "village" and which he knew well.

"MA-SU-MU-RA-*san*, is this how you write your name?"

MA-SU-MU-RA frowned, caught off guard.

"No," he said flatly. He didn't elaborate, keeping the secret of his name to himself.

BEN GAVE UP. IN HIS MEMORY, THE GUY WOULD FOREVER remain MA-SU-MU-RA, in *hiragana*. A few days later, Ben spotted, on the nameplate of a locker, the *kanji* for *mura* below a *kanji* he didn't know. But it was too late—like most Japanese words Ben encountered at that time, the name had already been etched onto his brain as *hiragana*. It had become yet another attribute of the guy, like his washed-out complexion and his cold, reticent demeanor.

MA-SU-MU-RA looked back and forth between Ben's face and his uniform one more time. Then he took another step back. He seemed to want to ask Ben a question in return, but he couldn't find the right form of address. Without using Ben's name, which he had just learned, or any of the Japanese words for "you"—*anata, kimi*, or *omae*—MA-SU-MU-RA pointed his chin toward the spot where Ben was standing and tossed him a question.

"America?"

This time, Ben was the one who fell silent. To avoid MA-SU-MU-RA's eyes, which had zeroed in on him, Ben looked at the wide staircase leading from the mezzanine down to the first floor.

Don't you have anything else to ask about me?

Ben said nothing for a few seconds, fixing his eyes on the glass door down below, looking for an answer that was not there. His own face went as blank as MA-SU-MU-RA's. Finally, annoyed by MA-SU-MU-RA's increasingly skeptical gaze, Ben mumbled, "*Ee*." Yeah. It occurred to Ben that a suspect might make the same kind of half-hearted admission during a forced confession: *ee*, after all, was definitely not the same thing as "yes."

As though he had been waiting for Ben's response, MA-SU-MU-RA quickly shot back, "Well, I hate America."

MA-SU-MU-RA said this devoid of emotion. But there was life in his voice for the first time. It had conviction, at least to Ben's ears. Once again MA-SU-MU-RA moved his eyes from Ben's face down to Ben's Cassle uniform, then squared his shoulders, as though readying himself for a fight.

"I don't much like it myself," Ben replied.

The white jacket of the uniform, which MA-SU-MU-RA was glaring at, felt nice and tight around Ben's torso.

Look, MA-SU-MU-RA-san, I'm just like you.

MA-SU-MU-RA seemed puzzled for a moment and then asked in a tone of voice more like a comeback than a question, "New York?"

Ben sensed a certain sticky persistence in MA-SU-MU-RA's voice. His question didn't sound like it meant "Were you born in New York?" or "Are you from New York?" Instead, it sounded like, do you belong to the place called New York? You're not supposed to be here, so where are you really supposed to be—is it the place called New York?

Ben imagined Japanese police officers using the same tone of voice when they interrogated people. He fell silent again.

MA-SU-MU-RA stared straight at Ben, still waiting for an answer. At that moment, MA-SU-MU-RA's pallid face looked tougher than it had before. His thin lips began to move, as if to say, "Okay, I'll ask you this one more time." But then, MA-SU-MU-RA suddenly changed position and shouted to the foot of the wide staircase, "*Arigatō gozaimashita.*" Thank you for coming.

Looking in the direction where MA-SU-MU-RA had shouted, Ben saw an older man in an overcoat and a twenty-something woman, who looked to be a hostess, heading toward the glass door.

At the last minute, Ben yelled down to the first floor at the top of his lungs, "*Arigatō gozaimashita.*" Overlaid with MA-SU-MU-RA's voice, Ben's high-pitched, strained voice echoed off the walls of Cassle. The woman who looked like a hostess turned back. As soon as she noticed Ben standing next to MA-SU-MU-RA at the top of the stairs, she pulled on the sleeve of the older man's overcoat and pointed. She whispered something into the older man's ear, and they burst out laughing. They continued laughing all the way out the door.

The sounds of the side street came in through the open door. Carried along by the side street, the noise from the plaza flowed in as well.

From amid the noise, the unbelievably clear voice of a woman's singing floated up to Ben. He couldn't make out the lyrics at all. Nobody else in Cassle seemed to be paying any attention to her. Ben remembered the poster of the woman who proudly gazed down like a queen upon the entrance to the plaza the evening after he arrived in SHIN-JU-KU. He got lost in the fantasy that it was her voice that was flowing so graciously from the plaza to the side street.

"New York?"

MA-SU-MU-RA's nagging voice interrupted Ben's reverie.

On MA-SU-MU-RA's expressionless face, there was now a clear look of anticipation.

In Ben's head, the words "New York" no longer signified a place where his relatives lived; it was just a meaningless string of *katakana*.

MA-SU-MU-RA-san, I don't wanna talk about New York. I don't wanna talk in katakana. *This is SHIN-JU-KU, remember?*

MA-SU-MU-RA's mouth began to move again.

The woman's voice vanished from Ben's mind. He got scared.

Anywhere will do, just name a place.

"Washington . . . D.C.," Ben said.

No sooner had the words left Ben's mouth than MA-SU-MU-RA quickly fired back: "Never heard of it."

His voice had an almost conceited ring to it.

Shifting his gaze away from Ben, MA-SU-MU-RA picked up a cloth and, with a burst of sudden energy, began buffing the ashtrays lined up on the counter.

Ben eyed MA-SU-MU-RA suspiciously, wondering how the guy could forget about him so quickly and throw himself into his work like that. He felt like he was beginning to understand why MA-SU-MU-RA had hounded him so much.

Never heard of it. MA-SU-MU-RA no doubt wanted the opportunity to say that. MA-SU-MU-RA might have known a lot more than he let on. For him, though, ignorance must have been the only place he could feel at home.

"A customer," MA-SU-MU-RA mumbled, as though talking to himself, and automatically picked up a glass of water and an ashtray from atop the counter. With brisk steps, he carried them over to the table where a man in a suit had just sat down. Ben listened carefully to MA-SU-MU-RA saying *nani ni itashimasu ka* ("What may I bring you?") and *kashikomarimashita* ("My pleasure") in a loud, booming voice. Then he watched closely as MA-SU-MU-RA went down the wide staircase. MA-SU-MU-RA may have been ugly, but his meticulous, precise movements acquired a kind of beauty in Ben's eyes. In Cassle, conduct was king. Unless he learned to conduct himself like MA-SU-MU-RA, Ben realized, he wouldn't survive long there. Ben was so engrossed in MA-SU-MU-RA's conduct that only when the guy was gone did he realize that all of the customers on the mezzanine were staring at him.

As he realized this, a chorus of *irasshaimase* ("welcome") rang out from the first floor, followed by two more customers coming up the stairs. When they spotted Ben in his uniform, the customers seemed confused and looked around. Relieved to find other customers sitting around the room normally, they sat down tentatively at an open table.

Ben saw only the confusion on their faces. Without looking at the customers, he lowered his eyes, paralyzed for a moment.

Then, bracing himself, he lowered his high-pitched voice like MA-SU-MU-RA had done and said, "*Irasshaimase.*"

Just as MA-SU-MU-RA had done, he picked up two glasses and an ashtray. With the same brisk steps as MA-SU-MU-RA, he marched over to the customers, keeping his eyes straight ahead. Trying not to look at their faces, he fixed his eyes on a calendar on the wall above their heads and plunked the glasses and the ashtray down in front of them.

Before any looks of surprise could surface on the two faces gazing up at him, Ben asked in a strong and clear voice, "*Nani ni itashimasu ka.*"

Perhaps he had said it perfectly, for below him he sensed the customers' eyes shifting from his face to the menus. As though the person standing there was not Ben but MA-SU-MU-RA, one of the customers simply muttered, "Let's see, spaghetti with meat sauce and a lemon tea."

"A coffee," the other customer said. That's when Ben realized that the second customer was a woman.

"*Kashikomarimashita.*"

The customers never uttered the word *gaijin*, perhaps because the tone of his voice—firm but not too loud, just like MA-SU-MU-RA's—shielded him from it.

Just as Ben turned his back to the mezzanine, he thought he heard a number of whispers erupt behind him. On his way down the stairs, he passed MA-SU-MU-RA coming up with a cup of coffee on a tray. MA-SU-MU-RA said nothing.

MA-SU-MU-RA-san, I'm gonna beat you at your own game.

When he reached the bottom, Ben saw the Manager standing like a sentinel at the far end, near the kitchen. Like backlighting, the harsh glare from the strong fluorescent lights and the yellow steam wrapped around the Manager. Behind him, Ben saw three men at work, their aprons covered with stains, beneath the blinding light that seemed to say "keep out" if you had no business there.

Ben walked right up to the Manager and recited his order loud and clear without any slip-ups, like an actor spitting out his hard-learned lines: "I got one spaghetti with meat sauce, one coffee, and one lemon tea."

The Manager immediately turned back to the kitchen and yelled, "*Wan miito wan hotto wan reti.*"

Wan, wan, wan. He sounded like a dog barking.

The moment the Manager let loose the stream of sounds in *katakana*, the men in aprons glanced in Ben's direction but kept working under the yellow-white light, without doing a double take.

Trying not to drop the *wan miito wan hotto wan reti* from the tray, Ben returned to the second floor. Like MA-SU-MU-RA, he placed them on the table and said, *O-matase itashimashita* ("Sorry to keep you waiting"). He could feel MA-SU-MU-RA's silence on his back from the opposite table, which MA-SU-MU-RA was wiping down. Two more customers came into the restaurant. Almost simultaneously, as though competing with each other, Ben and MA-SU-MU-RA both shouted, *Irasshaimase*. Ben got to the table before MA-SU-MU-RA and took the order, the words rolling off his tongue with surprising clarity. Then he went back downstairs.

This time, when he reached the first floor, the Manager was nowhere in sight.

Ben walked slowly toward the harsh light coming from the kitchen. Stopping, he stood there alone.

In the kitchen, he could see the men who were busily preparing the food, paying no attention to him. Two were older than Ben, but one—an apprentice perhaps—was a young guy about the same age.

The apprentice looked up from a big pot and stared blankly at Ben. He had a chubby face. It displayed neither friendliness nor malice—not even curiosity. It was just a chubby yellow face under the fluorescent lights. Seeing Ben standing there by himself, he seemed to say, "Well, what is it?"

Not sure where he found the courage, Ben wrenched his voice from deep in his abdomen and yelled, "*Tsū hotto wan miito wan tōsuto.*" Two coffees, one spaghetti with meat sauce, one toast.

From the yellow-white light, a voice flew back at him:

"Comin' right up."

It was a cheerful voice. It was an uninhibited voice, the kind you might use to anyone.

BEN LIKED WORKING THE NIGHT SHIFT. FOR EIGHTY yen, or about twenty cents, an hour, it was a lot of work, but he never found it particularly arduous. As he stood on the mezzanine of Cassle, the changing faces of SHIN-JU-KU would appear one after another over the course of a night. He considered himself lucky to be in the middle of it all. He got the feeling that SHIN-JU-KU was coming to him for free, putting on a show for his benefit.

He liked the sound of the mournful Japanese ballads oozing from the cable radio, which the Manager turned on and off according to whim, and the sweet, sharp odor rising from the Hi-Lite and Short Peace cigarettes around the room. He liked the sound of *hiragana* flying back and forth when the employees called to one another: MA-SU-MU-RA on the mezzanine and YA-SU-DA-*kun* on the first floor, the cooks, I-SHI-GU-RO-*san* and SA-TŌ-*san*, and the apprentice, TA-CHI-BA-NA (for some reason, only Ben was called by his given name, Ben, not his surname, Isaac, and nobody added the familiar suffix -*kun* to his name, much less the polite suffix -*san*).

More than anything else, Ben liked seeing the different kinds of customers that came in every time the glass door opened. The customer base of Cassle changed quite a bit depending on the time of night. In the early evening hours after eight o'clock, when Ben started work, most of the customers were couples and groups of young people who drifted over from the nearby jazz cafés and go-go clubs. The voices of students spouting English words like "outsider" or French names like Lévi-Strauss would sometimes reach Ben's ears on the mezzanine from the group section on the first floor. From midnight or so onward, the majority were businessmen who had missed the last train home. Even if they came in groups of two or three, they rarely engaged in conversation, perhaps because they had run out of things to talk about. Nursing their beers and nibbling at their plates of curry rice, they would quietly bury their noses in manga like intoxicated teenage boys.

Then, after two o'clock, in marked contrast to the gray impression left on the mezzanine by the mute businessmen, the so-called "water-trade customers"—people who worked in the local bars and brothels—would parade in, showing off their colorful attire. Overweight *mama-san*s would bring in hostesses decked out in pink and lavender evening gowns. When their loud laughter hit the stairs, it seemed to Ben that Cassle had been transformed into a palace. There were thirty-something women wearing miniskirts in December and young men sporting tropical-colored neckties. There was even a middle-aged man who, like Ringo Starr without a pinkie, wore rings on his remaining nine fingers. Conversations of people spilling industry secrets in loud voices—thinking Ben wouldn't understand them—sprang up across the mezzanine, along with scenes of people openly exchanging bundles of cash right under Ben's nose—thinking it was none of his business.

Then, after three o'clock, Cassle quieted down again, the party ending as quickly as it had begun, and the remaining customers nodded off to sleep, slumped over uncomfortably in their small chairs. That was the slowest time of night, the time right before they got ready to close, when all the employees could do was wait for the predawn light from the plaza to steal in through the glass door, which hardly opened anymore.

All night long, MA-SU-MU-RA stood on the opposite side of the counter, averting his eyes from Ben as much as possible and saying nothing other than the few words needed to do their jobs. Although MA-SU-MU-RA stood next to him in stony silence, Ben enjoyed eavesdropping on the various customers' conversations, so he never felt particularly lonely. Ben spent his nights thus—stuck between a wall of silence a few feet away and a world of colorful Japanese a few yards away.

A LITTLE PAST ONE O'CLOCK IN THE MORNING AFTER A few nights on the job—during the quiet interlude after the businessmen finished ordering and before the "water-trade customers" poured in—Ben noticed for the first time that MA-SU-MU-RA was reading a book. Ben didn't know if MA-SU-MU-RA had brought it in that night to avoid having to talk to him or had been reading it as a way to pass the time when business was slow, but MA-SU-MU-RA was poring over a thick book on the counter. There was something about the side of MA-SU-MU-RA's face hunched over the book, completely absorbed in it, that made Ben think of those haggard profiles of monks in medieval Europe devoutly studying the Bible.

As he watched him, Ben realized something odd. MA-SU-MU-RA seemed to be reading the same part over and over, hardly ever turning the book's pages.

Wondering if it was a difficult book, Ben peeked over MA-SU-MU-RA's slender shoulder at the open page crammed with Japanese characters. There were a few *kanji* he recognized, but the sentences he saw made no sense to him.

When he noticed Ben's prying eyes, MA-SU-MU-RA slammed the book shut.

But Ben was able to catch a glimpse of the book's gray cover, which was without any illustration. He'd seen a book like it somewhere. Maybe it was the same book he often spotted at the bookstore near W University that Andō took him to during the autumn—the "hard book everyone's readin'," as Andō said. The cover was the same color as the sky back then. The *kanji* for the name Yoshimoto was embossed on the cover, followed by two *kanji* Ben couldn't read.

"What kind of book is that?" Ben asked, his eyes stuck on the illegible *kanji*.

Mind your own business, MA-SU-MU-RA seemed to say, stepping back, clutching the book in one hand. At pains to reply, he said in a low voice, "You guys wouldn't understand."

For a moment, Ben was left speechless.

It wasn't that he was shocked to hear he "wouldn't understand." Truth be told, he probably wouldn't understand at all. What took Ben by surprise was suddenly being referred to in the plural as "you guys."

He decided not to ask anything more about the book.

MA-SU-MU-RA carefully opened the book on the counter farthest from Ben and returned to his reading pose, all the while monitoring Ben's movements out of the corner of his eye.

What sorts of secrets were inscribed in the Yoshimoto book? For MA-SU-MU-RA, it was probably a domain completely off limits to Ben, or maybe it was a talisman to protect him from Ben. At the same time, as Ben watched the way MA-SU-MU-RA shielded the book from view by thrusting out his slender shoulders, he couldn't help but think that MA-SU-MU-RA was trying to keep the book away from him, not the other way around. As if the book would burst into flame if it ever came into contact with Ben's eyes.

MEALTIME FOR THE EMPLOYEES AT CASSLE WAS AROUND 3:30 a.m., after the "water-trade customers" had left.

Despite having only a cream-filled roll and two bean-jam doughnuts in the evening before work, Ben didn't feel that hungry for the first few days, perhaps because the time he spent in Cassle was so interesting. One night, though, after taking the last order from the "water-trade customers," Ben picked up his meal from the cook, SA-TŌ-san, and the apprentice, TA-CHI-BA-NA, and carried it up to the mezzanine. Seeing this, the Manager pointed to his potbelly and chuckled, "Ee-to, ee-to, foo-do, foo-do," excited to try out his own English on Ben. When the Manager chanted those words, Ben suddenly felt his appetite return.

The next night, Ben and MA-SU-MU-RA happened to sit down across from each other at one end of a long, narrow table in the group section. Soon after they sat down, the apprentice cook, TA-CHI-BA-NA, brought them their meals on plastic trays. Bringing his own tray out last, TA-CHI-BA-NA sat down next to MA-SU-MU-RA.

Over the past few nights, Ben had conveyed dozens of orders to TA-CHI-BA-NA from the entrance of the kitchen. Each time, TA-CHI-BA-NA showed no particular surprise at Ben's existence. Sure enough, though, when the easygoing guy finally sat down right across from Ben, he looked back and forth between his face and his uniform, just as MA-SU-MU-RA had done the first time he laid eyes on Ben.

During those nights, Ben had gotten into the habit of looking down whenever people stared at him. He did so again now.

Undeterred, TA-CHI-BA-NA asked, "So how old are you?"

Ben raised his eyes and glanced at TA-CHI-BA-NA's chubby, boyish face. The look he saw in TA-CHI-BA-NA's eyes was different than MA-SU-MU-RA's on his first night.

"Uh, seven . . . teen."

"You're seventeen? Same as me then."

In his head, Ben subtracted seventeen from forty-two, calculating what year he was born in the Shōwa era. Just as he was about to announce this, MA-SU-MU-RA—who had been listening quietly from the side—blurted out in a loud voice, "*Sebunteen.*"

Stressing the *s* like the hiss of a snake, MA-SU-MU-RA's sibilance seeped into every nook and cranny of Cassle.

"*Eye yamu sssebunteen eears ol-doh.*"

MA-SU-MU-RA was too serious to be making a joke. With one look from TA-CHI-BA-NA, he shut up.

Ben looked down again.

Right in front of him sat a big bowl of rice and a plate holding a mountain of shredded cabbage next to a fish with red skin.

It was a kind of fish he had never seen before. Like so many things in the world around him, Ben didn't know the name of it.

MA-SU-MU-RA and TA-CHI-BA-NA probably knew the name of the fish. But Ben didn't feel like asking them. He didn't want to see what he looked like to MA-SU-MU-RA asking such a dumb question.

Ben pulled apart the wooden chopsticks. Ben held his chopsticks differently than MA-SU-MU-RA and TA-CHI-BA-NA, who were already digging in across from him. Unlike the proper way of holding them—inserting the two chopsticks between the thumb and index finger and moving them up and down to pick up pieces of food—he turned them sideways like scissors. Ben knew it was a weird way to hold them, but he could pick up even a single grain of rice if he put his mind to it, so he never had any troubles.

Ben had learned to hold his chopsticks like that from the *yongren* who lived in the outbuilding behind the house in Taiwan where he lived when he was a kid. Was this the way the *yongren* themselves held them, or was this Ben's clumsy imitation of the way the *yongren* held them? Or was it possible the *yongren* were too lazy to teach Ben the right way to hold them, thinking it was a lost cause? Ben didn't know anymore. He had a vague memory of his father making fun of him for holding them "like a Chinese coolie," but when he went "home" to America after that, he never had the chance to correct the habits of his youth.

Seeing Ben using his chopsticks that way, MA-SU-MU-RA nudged TA-CHI-BA-NA with his elbow and pointed to Ben with his chin. Unlike MA-SU-MU-RA's demeaning gaze—which seemed proud to uncover yet another niggling detail about Ben—TA-CHI-BA-NA's eyes were filled with childish wonder, as though captivated by the activity of a rare animal.

Two very different kinds of light were coming from the four Japanese eyes looking at him. Ben looked down at the food on the plastic tray. There was a whole fish in front of him—a fish with no name, a fish with tender red skin.

He raised his chopsticks and wielded them like scissors, attacking the fish ferociously. Grasping the loosened chunks of red skin and white meat between his chopsticks, he quickly stuffed them into his mouth so as not to drop anything.

Almost immediately, Ben choked and spat. "Ahh," he cried out, spewing bits and pieces of fish onto his plate. Big and small bones glistened.

MA-SU-MU-RA and TA-CHI-BA-NA were watching wide-eyed.

A tiny bone had got caught in his throat, making him choke. Ben wanted to kill himself right then and there.

Unable to stay quiet any longer, TA-CHI-BA-NA exclaimed, "Cut it like this," and ran his chopsticks along the backbone of the fish on his plate, cutting it neatly and evenly in half.

"Thanks," Ben gasped, incredibly grateful.

He cleared his throat and wiped his mouth with the wet towel. Imitating TA-CHI-BA-NA, he thrust his chopsticks into the spine of the fish and tried to pull them along the backbone. But they got caught on a rib and ended up cutting a jagged line through the red skin.

"No, cut it like this."

As Ben poked around with his chopsticks, TA-CHI-BA-NA reached over to help him. But suddenly, from the right, MA-SU-MU-RA intercepted TA-CHI-BA-NA's hand in midair.

"Don't waste your time."

TA-CHI-BA-NA pulled his hand back, silent.

"I told you, he's not like you and me, so don't waste your time."

Ben looked down once again.

Having finished his meal first, MA-SU-MU-RA lit up a Hi-Lite with a smug look on his face, then left the table.

TA-CHI-BA-NA glanced over at downcast Ben before taking off after MA-SU-MU-RA.

Alone in the group section, Ben continued to eat, using his fingers to pick out the tiny bones one by one from the fish sawed in half on his plate. Taking their turn, SA-TŌ-san and YA-SU-DA-kun sat across from Ben and had their meals. The whole time, Ben never looked up. It wasn't until after they'd gone that Ben finally finished eating his fish.

When he was done, he brought the rice bowl to his lips and shoveled the remaining rice into his mouth all at once, as the yongren had taught him to do.

EARLY ONE MORNING, A WEEK OR SO INTO THE JOB, BEN was summoned to the first floor by the Manager after cleaning the toilet in preparation for closing. Pointing at TA-CHI-BA-NA, who was carrying out plastic bags of garbage from the kitchen, the Manager ordered Ben to help: "Gomi, out-o." Trash, outside. With both hands, Ben lifted up a large bag—its contents sloshing around—and pushed open the kitchen door with one foot. Stepping outside, he found himself in a back alley. The alley was lined with hostess bars, massage parlors, and hole-in-the-wall restaurants. On the corner stood TA-CHI-BA-NA in his apron.

TA-CHI-BA-NA had just dropped a black trash bag onto a mountain of other trash bags and was pushing it in with the tip of his wooden clog. When he saw Ben, he called out, "Over here." Dragging the black plastic bag across the paving stones, Ben got it to where TA-CHI-BA-NA was standing and, in the same way, kicked it onto the mountain of trash with his loafer.

From behind, the sound of light footsteps, like a pack of small animals scurrying away, echoed across the paving stones. Ben and TA-CHI-BA-NA turned their heads simultaneously.

Midway down the alley, under an unlit neon sign in *kanji* that Ben couldn't read, several women appeared one after another and then hurried off in the opposite direction. In the dim light of the alley, the hems of their garish gowns flashed from under their dark coats. As they got farther away, they turned to the left and dashed out of sight, toward the train station.

The sound of the first train reached the alley and then all was quiet once again.

MA-SU-MU-RA came out the kitchen door with YA-SU-DA-*kun*, from the first floor, behind him. They blithely tossed their plastic bags onto the mountain of trash. MA-SU-MU-RA then lit a cigarette and lingered in the middle of the alley without saying a word. Neither YA-SU-DA-*kun* nor TA-CHI-BA-NA made any attempt to return to Cassle.

Staring deep into the alley, MA-SU-MU-RA began walking, as though something had caught his eye. He stopped in front of a darkened restaurant next to where the women had come out.

The predawn light from the plaza was just beginning to creep into the alley, but the inner reaches were still bathed in shadows. Ben fixed his eyes there. Like a replacement for the mountain of trash heaped on the corner, containers of what looked to be freshly delivered foodstuffs were stacked beside the lattice door of the restaurant where MA-SU-MU-RA now stood.

Looking around to make sure no other people were in the alley, MA-SU-MU-RA put out his cigarette on the paving stones and opened the top container. In the pale light, dozens of white eggs were sitting in the container.

MA-SU-MU-RA picked up an egg. Looking around one more time, he swiftly cracked it open on his knee—as fast as a magician, Ben marveled—and then poured the contents into his mouth. The white shell fell onto the paving stones with a crack.

With a wave that said, "Come on, you guys," MA-SU-MU-RA called YA-SU-DA-*kun* and TA-CHI-BA-NA over. Ben, of course, knew that gesture didn't include him. He stood where he was, keeping his eyes on YA-SU-DA-*kun* and TA-CHI-BA-NA as they walked over to MA-SU-MU-RA.

Just like MA-SU-MU-RA had done, YA-SU-DA-*kun* took an egg from the container, cracked it open, and brought it to his lips, swallowing the stuff without spilling a drop.

TA-CHI-BA-NA then stooped over and cracked open an egg on the tip of his wooden clog. Then, in similar fashion, he brought the egg up to his mouth and downed its contents in one gulp.

From the corner, Ben gazed at the quick, elegant movements being performed over and over by the three guys in white uniforms in the deserted alley.

Just the thought of a raw egg made Ben feel queasy.

A ray of light from the plaza shot into the alley, boldly highlighting the paving stones but stopping short of the three men's feet.

As he stood there alone on the corner in the growing light, Ben suddenly had a sinking feeling that the three guys in the shadows had turned their eyes upon him all at once. At the center of the single white mass formed by the three guys in their uniforms, he could make out MA-SU-MU-RA's moving lips:

"Bet you guys can't do this."

MA-SU-MU-RA's challenge echoed through the alley, his voice almost hostile.

Ben instinctively looked over his shoulder. There was no one.

For Chrissake, who are all these guys you keep seeing behind me?!

The figures of the three guys were completely still, as though locked in a standoff with Ben. From within the shadows, he caught only the sound of YA-SU-DA-*kun* snickering.

Ben was seized by an indescribable emotion, something resembling anger yet different. Driven by an unknown force, he stepped forward onto the paving stones and marched right up to the three guys. Avoiding MA-SU-MU-RA, he reached out his hand to the container and grabbed an egg.

MA-SU-MU-RA stepped back farther into the alley.

Smash it in his fucking face!

The thought raced through Ben's mind in English, but his momentary turmoil soon subsided.

Ben cracked the egg open on the metal shutter of the restaurant. Parts of it stuck to the shutter, some fluid landing on the collar of his uniform. When he brought the cracked egg up to his face, a rising sun floating in the translucent liquid loomed before his eyes. He promptly dumped the contents into his mouth.

For a split second, the inside of the alley became as bright as day.

Feeling like he might throw up, Ben gagged on the sticky substance coating the roof of his mouth and the insides of his throat, but he forced himself to swallow.

Ben's eyes met MA-SU-MU-RA's, which were gleaming dimly in the depths of the alley. There was no expression in MA-SU-MU-RA's eyes. Like the first night they met, he just stared in Ben's direction with no expression whatsoever.

Looking away first, Ben turned his back on the three guys and began running. Just as he stepped through the kitchen door into Cassle, he thought he heard TA-CHI-BA-NA cheer, "Way to go!" From the kitchen, he ran by the register—where the Manager was thumbing through a stack of receipts—up to the mezzanine, and then past the DŌ-HAN-SHI-TSU. When he came to the dressing room on the third floor, he realized he was trembling. He tore off the uniform, which was covered in stains from the collar to the thighs.

Ben's voice echoed off the walls of the empty dressing room: "*Hazukashii.*" Humiliating.

Opening the only locker without a nametag on it, he saw his flannel shirt and jeans hanging inside.

Ben looked up.

The early morning light of SHIN-JU-KU was coming in through the air vent. The light was hitting his bare white arm. His mind drifted back to that autumn evening when Andō had pointed to the distant lights and told him, "That's SHIN-JU-KU."

It was just light streaming through the air vent, nothing more than the pale light of dawn.

His trembling suddenly stopped. Ben slowly changed back into his American clothes. After he had put the soiled uniform away in the locker, he stood on the landing once again and looked down the long staircase. Below him was the marble staircase of the consulate. He saw the small, slippery stone steps from the morning he first set foot in Shinjuku.

Ben stood on the landing, unable to move.

The Manager was no longer at the register. Ben crept down the stairs. Cutting across the first floor, he quietly headed toward the glass door.

The reflection of the pale white *gaijin* face in the glass door grew bigger and bigger. Closing his eyes, Ben pushed the face aside and walked out.

NOTES

TRANSLATOR'S INTRODUCTION

1. Zhouliu Wu, *Orphan of Asia*, trans. Ioannis Mentzas (New York: Columbia University Press, 2006) and Kim Sŏk-pŏm, *The Curious Tale of Mandogi's Ghost*, trans. Cindi Textor (New York: Columbia University Press, 2010).

2. Ōe Kenzaburō, "Koe no buntai: sōgo rikai no hashiwatashi ni naru fukusū no gengo de ikiru keiken" (Literary voices: the experience of living in multiple languages as a bridge to mutual understanding), *Asahi Shinbun*, 23 April 1992, evening edition.

3. Levy Hideo, "Hajimete no Nihongo" (My first time in Japanese), *Seijōki no kikoenai heya* (A room where the star-spangled banner cannot be heard) (Tokyo: Kōdansha, 2004), 162.

A ROOM WHERE

THE STAR-SPANGLED BANNER CANNOT BE HEARD

1. Japanese acronym for the 1951 U.S.–Japan Security Treaty. The renewal of this treaty sparked widespread protests during the 1950s and 1960s.

2. "Shōwa 3—Commemoration of Imperial Accession": a memorial to the enthronement of the Shōwa emperor (Hirohito) on November 10, 1928.

1. "Only ¥1,000."

2. "Smash the Security Treaty" and "Restore the Shōwa Emperor."

TRANSLATOR'S ACKNOWLEDGMENTS

FIRST, I WOULD LIKE TO THANK LEVY-SAN FOR WRITING THIS NOVEL and allowing me to translate it into English. I can only hope that my translation lives up to his high expectations and the poetry of the original. I also wish to thank the Japanese Literature Publishing Project, especially Ogawa Yasuhiko and Chris Braham, for commissioning this translation and seeing it through to publication. Jennifer Crewe and Elmer Luke provided expert editorial advice at different stages of this project. Adrienne Hurley, Kō Young-ran, Kōno Kensuke, Christine Marran, Peter Rachleff, Jim Reichert, Ann Sherif, John Treat, Atsuko Ueda, and Melissa Wender have inspired and encouraged my work in various ways. Special thanks to Indra Levy for organizing the symposium "Japanese in the World" at Stanford University in February 2010 and for being so supportive. Students in my courses "Translating Japanese: Theory and Practice" and "Race and Ethnicity in Japan" at Macalester College read and commented on earlier drafts of the translation. Without my parents, Richard and Margaret Scott, I would never have gone to Japan and learned Japanese in the first place. Finally, Weishiun (Andy) Tsai has stood by me through thick and thin, for which I have no words to express my gratitude.